Carol x

BIG TWISTS LITTLE TALES

An anthology of twenty five short stories and poetry
by Jessica Fairfax and Carol Walker

thank you

Jess x

A **FairWalk** Production

Cover design and photography by Carol Walker and Jessica Fairfax.

First Print
2017

BIG TWISTS LITTLE TALES is a diverse collection of stories, with surprises.
There will be violence, swearing and humour, albeit dark, but it aims to entertain.

All Characters are works of fiction, a product of the author's fertile (and dark) imagination. Any resemblance to actual people, living or dead, or actual events is purely coincidental
(although some may have provided inspiration).

Contents

Introduction

Jessica Fairfax and Carol Walker write individually and together. This Anthology has been a long time coming. It's an insight to how they both think and is a celebration of the stories they love to read and tell. They will lead you by the hand down some alleyways you may not have travelled before.

BIG TWISTS LITTLE TALES is a collection of short stories which have dark undertones and surprises with some unexpected twists.

This is a perfect read to relax with a cup of coffee, an escapism over lunch in the middle of your busy day or to help you pass the time on a journey. It's designed for you to be able to dip in and out and, hopefully, give you the odd chill or uncomfortable thrill.

We hope you enjoy reading them as much as we have enjoyed writing them.

Temperature Rising

The clock ticks annoyingly; drumming in rhythm. I wake through a fog; not with a start but uncomfortably slow. The room is eerie, quiet and still. A pale yellow glow hovers from a small light in the corner. There's a crack in the thin, pale blue curtains and it's dark outside; it's the middle of the night. What woke me up? Was it the clock? I have a vague recollection of a dream, it escapes me. I'm confused.

There's a slight smell of electricity burning in the atmosphere. As my eyes get used to the dark, the deep black fades to a midnight blue. My eyes are grainy and itchy. It's difficult to focus. I try to look around, all I can see are pale green double doors with round, porthole windows. They look solid, heavy, with no handles.

My head's full of cotton wool balls. I'm on the verge of a real thought as a nurse breezes in through the doors.

"Good, you're awake," she said, "We've all been worried about you. How are you feeling?"

I try to speak, to reply and nothing comes out, my lips are numb. I want to ask her where I am.
She doesn't look at me. She walks purposefully over to the corner of the room where there's a trolley. I try to ask again, who is she and why I am here but I have no voice. She's either ignoring me, or she doesn't realise I am trying to speak to her.

"That was some explosion, you are lucky to be alive," she says.
Explosion! What explosion? The word reverberates. I can't remember. I can't move; I'm pinned to the bed. This must be what shock feels like. I try to sit up so I can see her better but I can't. My body is stiff, sore and my head pounds to the beat of my pulse.
"There are fourteen of you found alive so far," she continues.
I attempt to thrash against the bed, in a bid to move. She still doesn't look at me.
"It was a nasty one this time," she says. "Gas they think. The whole place went up in a huge blast. At least three of the twelve tunnels have been taken out. That's never been known in the Earsden pit."
I gasp, and stop my struggle.

"They aren't sure how many men were in the pit. The rescue team are working round the clock."
It's very hard to breathe. I feel warm, hot. I could do with a window open. I can hear my own shallow breath, there isn't enough air. My chest is crushing under an invisible weight. I can hear the tinkle of metal objects being gently placed into metal trays, like small bells ringing.

"Everyone is gathered at the pit head, hoping amongst hope. Total despair," she shakes her head.
It can't be, it's impossible. I remember … I remember … No it's gone. I must have just arrived at work, maybe in the lift heading down the mine shaft. A routine I'd been through a thousand times before. There would have been a few of us in the cage.

"Your wife was here earlier, she said to tell you she will be back later."
What wife? I don't have a wife, do I? What does she mean? My God, I'm not sure anymore. Why can't I remember? The nurse is putting tablets in to little plastic cups. That's it! Maybe it's the drugs they've given me. *That's* why I can't remember!

I can hear the rustle of the starched cotton of her modern, pale blue dress, which flares out from her waist to her knees, as the nurse walks across the room. She'll see my distress now.

She approaches my bed. Taking a glass thermometer from the top pocket of her dress, she shakes it gently.
"Come now Mr Johnson, time for your medicine and let me check your temperature."
Mr Johnson? What's she talking about? I'm sure I'm not Mr Johnson. What's my name? Why can't I remember? I'm wading through treacle. I feel like I'm going to cry but I hold back the tears. It's basic stuff, for God's sake. I can't even remember my name. Hold on … there's a thought … it's coming … I'm Masters … Bill Masters. Hallelujah! I remember.

"Open wide Mr Johnson."
There's that Johnson again. What is with her? She turns away from me. What the hell is happening? Why isn't she looking at me? Look at me, for goodness sake, please for the love of God. Am I not suffering here? The pain is spreading all over; my hands, up my legs, my body. It feels like every nerve is standing on end.

There's another bed, I didn't notice it. There's something wrong with my eyes; they're dry and I can't see properly. I still can't focus. I have very little peripheral vision. Someone's in the bed, but who?

I shiver, feeling clammy and the palms of my hands are sweating; my legs and feet begin to feel numb.

I hear a voice I recognise, coming from the other bed;
"Nurse, can I ask you please? Only I'm concerned."
Who is that? Why can't I remember? Ah-ha! It's Fred. I have worked alongside him for the past 25 years. I should remember. A nice fella. Never has a bad word to say about anyone.
"What's happened to my pal, can you tell me please? He was there with me when the explosion …" Fred chokes over his words.
The nurse hesitates, "We're not supposed to give out that information. What's he called and I will see what I can do?"
"Bill Masters."
The nurse looks away, "I'm very sorry he's been badly injured."
"How bad?"

"Maybe you should speak to the doctor. He might be able to give you more information."
"Please nurse? Please just let me know if he is going to be ok?"
"I'm sorry Mr Johnson. I'm really sorry, you need to speak to the doctor."

What? What's going on? I'm lying here, badly injured and she is ignoring me. She hasn't made one attempt to speak to me; to check if I am ok. I'm suffering. It's getting worse. The pain is intolerable. I think I'm about to pass out. I'm burning. Heat engulfs me, burning pain. I'm thirsty too. So bloody thirsty and she hasn't asked if I would like a drink. What about *my* medication, *my* pain killers, *my* water, *my* care? Can't she see that I am right here? Nurses are supposed to be caring, helpful and professional.

I want to raise my hand as quickly as I want to raise my voice, but I don't have time to try. Two porters clatter in to the room, struggling with a trolley; the wheels are moving in different directions. The nurse doesn't seem to notice, or if she does she doesn't react; she moves quietly about her work.

Swiftly and without fuss, I'm transferred on to the trolley with the sheet that has been covering me. What are you doing? Where are you taking me? I try to wriggle, wave my hand, anything to get their attention.

The trolley bangs through the doors as I am transported through the corridors. My feet feel cold and exposed. No one has noticed.

We push through another set of double doors. There is a loud crack as a door smacks in to the end of the trolley, the porters struggle to straighten it. It shudders, forcing pain through my ransacked body.

"What do we have here lads?" A man's voice bellows over the noise as we enter another room. One porter picks up a flip chart and scans it.

"A Bill Masters, from the explosion at Earsdon Pit."

"Let me at him then. Let's see what we've got," the man says and I hear him snapping on his rubber gloves.

He switches a light on and shines it at my face. I'm blinded temporarily by the brightness. The little vision I have is eroded. Then the man, I presume is a doctor, dressed in blue scrubs and a mask on his face, comes in to soft focus.

“Jesus,” the doctor’s eyes widen. He spins round, whips off his mask and gags. He wipes his forehead with the back of his gloved hand. “He must have taken the brunt of it. I’ve never seen burns so severe.”

The two porters grunt and look at me with mild interest then move back from the trolley.

The doctor peers closer, “And the smell. He doesn’t even have eyelids. Poor bugger.”

No eyelids! No fucking eyelids! I can’t believe it! What’s he saying that for?

“How could he live like that?” the doctor heaves a deep sigh.

Like what? What does he mean? How could I live like what?

“Just as well he didn’t survive.”

Didn’t survive! What is he talking about? I did survive. I am alive. I’m here. HERE! Look! Hell’s teeth man, look!

“There’s not much left of him, is there? His last few hours must have been torture.”

I am still here you know! STILL FUCKING HERE! I try to move to show them I’m still alive but I can’t, I’m paralysed. I’m petrified. This can’t be happening.

"It's getting late now lads, get a label on him and we'll deal with him first thing in the morning."
A porter walks over to the other side of the room and returns with a label on a piece of string.
"What shall I do, Doc? He hasn't got any toes."
"Tie it round his foot then."
"But … there's no feet, Doc!"
"The stump then … the stump that's left. I take it he does have a stump? It's ok we'll know which end to look."
Stump! No feet? I have no feet. No FEET! I feel panic rising in my chest. My heart is trumpeting in small rhythmic peeps, it's going to explode. My head is in a cocoon, it's numb.

I hear the suction of a sealed door open. The trolley glides in. It's cold, really cold. Stop! Help! What are you doing? Tears sting the back of my eyes and I know I'm going to cry.

No wait, you can't! But the heavy door closes with a thud. It's dark. Very dark. It's freezing.

And I'm still alive.

Wheels

It wasn't the best start to the week. I had been seeing this guy, Matt, for about a month. He was fun; we always had a good time. I didn't get to see him much because our shifts often clashed. I'm a nurse and he said he worked for a car manufacturing company. So, we met a handful of times and yeah, we were intimate.

He rang me and said he wanted to pick me up first thing and take me out for the day, after dropping a car off. A surprise he said. Well, it was a surprise. I had been in the car with him a few times and he never behaved as twattish as he did that particular day. I didn't see it coming and I'm usually a good judge of character.

He rolled up in a different car each time we went out. It was always a decent set of wheels, usually a cabriolet. A perk from work he said. Must be nice, I thought, as I just get a uniform, which isn't as sexy as it could be and a bit of a discount here and there.

This time he arrived in a white soft top; the roof down. I didn't think it was warm enough but at least it was sunny. The last time we went out we were soaked through before he *remembered* which button he needed to press to put the roof up!

I got in and off we went. Matt put his foot down all the way through Tynemouth Village, when all the kids were on their way to school!

The school crossing patrol officer, aka, the lollipop man, was standing in the middle of the road, with his stick extended, millimetres from where Matt screeched to a halt.
"Get out the way you stupid c…!"
"Matt! He's fine!"
"Wha…? Oh, for God's sake woman! He's a fucking menace … You're a fucking hazard mate … nearly hit my car with that soddin' pole. Arsehole!"

I could feel myself sinking down into my seat with embarrassment. I told him there was no need for it but he ignored me and carried on hurling abuse at the poor man, who was just doing his job.
"Come on, for fuck's sake! He's letting the whole of Tynemouth across; those kids were miles away … oh fucking COME ON!" The faces of the parents said it

all. A dad shouted back at him, reminding him children were within earshot. It didn't stop him.

“What is your problem? We haven't got to be anywhere!” I heard myself shouting out the words over his rants. “We need to be away from here woman. I have to drop the car off by nine and it's overheating!” he leaned so far out of the car, I thought he would fall out. I hoped he would.

“That's fuckin' bad lollypoppin' that mate! How's he still employed, he must be a hundred?” He got no response from me. Yet he carried on…

“How are you still employed? Let some young person have a go, will ya! Do you know how hard it is to get a job! Fuckin' old twat! Should have retired after the war.”

“Look, we can go now, those parents are hanging back.” I was wafting my hand in a forward motion. I couldn't get out of there quick enough.

“At long fuckin' last!” Matt accelerated at a ridiculous speed, the wheels screeched. He didn't even stop at the junction to turn right. Horns were sounding all around us and other vehicles had to break hard to avoid us.

"You are so ..." I was shaking.

"And you should keep your opinions to yourself when I'm driving woman!"

"Let me out!" I'd had enough. I had been a victim of road rage once or twice but only when I had been driving. Usually something to do with me forgetting to indicate, apparently… but there is no excuse for it!

"What? No … What are you doing? You mad bitch, don't be openin ..."

"Let me out!" That lollipop man had been *my* lollipop man, when I was at school. He was practically family!

"Ok, ok, for fucks sake! I've stopped. What's your problem?"

"*My* problem? You speed through the village like it's a race track, then abuse a kind old man …"

"He was a fuckin' hazard! He needs a walking stick, not a lollipop stick. Thinks he's still dealing with horse and carts, not wheels with engines. Causes more accidents if you ask me! I only said what everyone was thinkin'!"

"I wasn't thinking it! Then … then, you abuse me for challenging you!"

"Abuse? Challenging? Have you been reading one of them fuckin' feminist books? Oh my God! Those fucking women who cry abuse after every disagreement!" He tutted loudly then looked away from me.

"So, go on then."

"What?"

"Get out my car. I've had enough of you anyway, you're too demanding and you've only given me one blow job since we met. Go on then, get out. Go burn your bra! GET THE FUCK OUT OF THE CAR!"

"Going, don't worry. And your dick is so small, you were lucky I found it that one time!" I slammed his car door and off I stomped. He called me something, not sure what but it wouldn't have been complimentary.

The car sounded ropey behind me, as I walked away. He did a seven point turn, swore; stalled it twice, swore; crunched the gears, swore. He then sped off back the way we came, leaving me on the pavement, texting my mate Nikki to see if she wanted to meet me for a coffee. I felt disappointed but relieved. At least I had witnessed his dickishness, before things got serious.

I began to calm down and decided to head back to the village. I hoped the lollipop man didn't recognise me.

I decided to keep my head down. I was a bit freaked out.

I had been looking forward to our day out but I had no idea he was that aggressive. His behaviour was so different to the guy I'd been dating these last few weeks. If Nikki were free, she would tell me to forget him. 'He's clearly a wanker!' she'd say and she'd be right.

As I neared the crossing where this *experience* had begun, I noticed the difference from just twenty minutes earlier. The traffic was negligible and no school uniforms were being hurried along by stressed parents, with exotically bred dogs, cockersprockerpoos … whatever.

As my phone 'pinged', something visible in the road made me stop in my tracks. Actually it wasn't in the road, it was under a car. Matt's badly parked car. The crossing patrol stick … the lollipop was *under* his car!

Matt was nowhere to be seen and nor was the lollipop man. There was a gloopy, dark liquid oozing into the gutter. Blood. Being medically trained means I see a lot of bodily fluids and this was unmistakeable. I didn't hesitate. I got my mobile out of my bag to phone the emergency services and Nikki's message was on the screen. She was on her way to the new coffee place to meet me. I quickly texted her back, to come and meet me on the roadside.

It was a brief exchange of texts. The lollipop man was injured. Possibly dead! I dialled 999.

"Ambulance please ... and the police … and the fire service. Road accident. Maybe a murder … Hello? Hi, yes there's been a hit and … er, run. Except the car is parked. Yes parked … but it wouldn't have been at the time of the accident, obviously; it would have been moving then, at speed. How do I know it's a hit and run? There's someone under it. The car. Yes, under it. Badly injured at least but he's probably dead, I haven't looked yet. Well I'm sorry, I thought it best to ring straight away! It looks serious, there's blood everywhere. Gallons of it. I'm a nurse, so ...Yes a nurse. The lollipop man. Hit at speed I'd say, from my experience of road traffic accidents. No, I don't know if he's breathing, I can't get to him. I *can* reach his lollipop though if … No, no of course that isn't very helpful, I was just saying … My name? Samantha. My friends call me Sam though but don't tell my mother ha! Oh sorry, Samantha *Ward*, I live on Percy Road ..."

Two police cars, an ambulance and a fire engine all attended within minutes of my call; not to mention all the people who materialised, meerkat-ing at the scene. The quiet road had once again erupted into life.

I was being questioned by a rather handsome police officer, as Nikki came round the corner with two take away lattes and her very blonde and slinky dog, a Saluki, called Zelda. They both bounced over.
"Hi love, are you ok? Oh hi, I'm Nikki, officer. Sorry, only got two lattes." She turned to me, as if the police officer wasn't there. "Texted Leyton to see what we should do but he's at work. He texted back, while I was getting the coffees and he said you should phone an ambulance but I guess you knew that."

Nikki's husband is a paramedic and in any medical emergency it's Leyton or me, she calls. We have dealt with all sorts together but this was a first! We laughed. Not a big loud explosion of laughter but never the less, in hindsight, it was probably not the time to be light-hearted.

A firefighter and a paramedic were lying prone, under Matt's car, trying to reach the lollipop man. The paramedic called over to the police officer, who asked me to wait a moment and headed to the car to see what they had found.

"Oh God, I can't see a dead body, Sam." Nikki said, as she took a long drawn out sip from her cup. "It's bad enough hearing all about them from Leyton." I tried to offer reassurance, as we both stood looking on at the unfolding scene. Being a nurse I was used to hearing bad news. I knew that the amount of blood pooling at the kerb, from the injuries sustained by that poor man trapped underneath the car, did not look good.

The firefighter, the paramedic and the police officer, simultaneously looked over to me, as they all got to their feet. The expressions on their faces said it all. The police officer began walking back over to us, holding something. Nikki looked at me, then back at the police officer, "Isn't that a …?" Before I could look, I was taken by surprise, someone was shouting my name. A familiar male voice.

“Sam, Sam what’s going on?” It was Matt, doing a harried run-walk back down a side street, round the bend towards his parked car, and towards the chaos. He was carrying a full two litre bottle of water.
“You ran over the lollipop man!” I couldn’t think of anything else to say to him.
“What? The radiator needed water, it’s a bloody wreck. The lollipop man? What are you talking ab...?” Matt looked at the police officer, the fire and ambulance crews and stopped dead in his tracks. His face drained of colour, as if someone had pulled a plug out of his big toe.

“It’s his car!” I shrieked at the police officer and pointed to Matt.
“Er Sam, I think there might have been a mista…” Nikki was trying to say something but I was trying to tell the police officer about the road rage and me getting out of the car and slamming the door and how Matt had then screeched off in temper and murdered the lollipop man.

“Is this your vehicle Sir?” the police officer walked over to a statue of Matt. Well it was more of a swagger actually.
“Er, this car?” Matt’s eyebrows were raised almost to his receding hairline.
“Yes, it’s his car, he picked me up in it this morning …” The police officer held his hand up to me, as if stopping traffic.

My eyes were on Matt. Nikki’s were still transfixed on whatever the police officer was holding.

“So, you are a Mrs Cait Hardy are you, Sir?” the police officer smirked. Matt’s mouth opened and closed but no sound came out. He looked like he might run at one point but then thought better of it. The police officer took Matt aside.

I saw the firefighters talking to the ambulance crew and then they all looked over at me again. I gave them my solemn face, as I know how hard it is to be in the presence of such tragedy. The lollipop man must have been beyond anyone’s help. I watched as the paramedics got into their ambulance and drove away, leaving the firefighters to remove the bits and pieces from the undercarriage of Matt's, or rather, Mrs Cait Hardy's car.

I verbalised my observations to Nikki.
"I don't think so Sam, did you not see what that nice policeman was holding?" The police officer was talking to Matt in an officious way and was putting handcuffs on him. I couldn't see what he was holding, until he put it on the wall.
"Plus," said Nikki. "Isn't that the lollipop man walking over the road from the big school?"

Oh! I could feel my heart pushing into my breast bone and sweat forming on my top lip. I had made a mistake. The liquid under the car was from the squashed bottle of a red fruit drink. To be fair it did look like blood. They all thought it was from the lollipop man. Who had popped his stick under the car, while he nipped into the senior school for a cuppa. Apparently, he always did that. And still does. You'd think he would learn!

"At least Matt isn't a murderer," Nikki said in a way that was supposed to make *everything ok then.*

“No, he isn’t but he is a dickhead who steals cars and verbally abuses women and old men.” I sighed and took the first sip of my lukewarm latte.
She had her sympathetic face on but there was something in Nikki’s eyes …

“The coffee shop looks nice. I had a little look round while I was waiting for the drinks. Zeldy’s allowed in. Shall we go there for cake, I need the loo so ..?” She then burst out laughing. “Sorry Sam, but are you actually a qualified nurse? This whole thing was hilaaaarious … can’t wait to tell Leyton!”

I laughed too. Eventually. Luckily the police officer was really ok about it. Getting an arrest probably helped. Nice guy actually. Very nice. I have to go and get ready. He’s picking me up at 8pm; he has a lush convertible.

Number 22 Sutton Street

Chaos, pure chaos. My mind races as confusion takes over my body. The room feels like it's closing in around me. I struggle to form a clear thought from the depth of a very, dark haze.

I reach for the lamp and fall to my knees. Legs buckle as tears course down my cheeks.

"Let me help?" he says, rushing round the bed, reaching for the lamp. I listen and try to understand what he means. Chaos prevents comprehension. He reaches forward and touches me on the arm; a light, gentle touch, which once I would have cherished.

My mind screams, I simply say, "No!" in a low tone, unlike anything I have said before. He removes his hand and looks down at me with pain in his eyes. I'm unable to care. My own pain is so acute. My world is broken. I hear my own heart beat in my temples.

I hate the lies the most. Meeting another woman, falling in love with someone else - it happens. It's the constant flow of lies which makes me question everything; even my own sanity. The lies he so expertly covered up, he must have had MI5 training! Do I really know this man?

As he watches me, he's crying. I pack essentials I know he'll need. I swipe the bathroom cabinet into a plastic bag. In his holdall I place jeans, work trousers, shirts, not the ones that are too tight, obviously. Even now, I'm looking after him. As I pass him, he grabs me. I try to pull away but he's stronger, physically. He says he can't live without me. I'm his rock, his soulmate, his best friend, as well as his wife. What was I when he was with other women? Clearly nothing.

If I have an ounce of sympathy for him then I would feel a human connection, but I don't. Not anymore.

"I'm sorry," he holds onto my limp hands, "Please let me stay? I've done something stupid, I realise that. I've learned my lesson. I love you. It's only ever been you." I pause and look at him. It's then that the idea comes.

"Ok," I say, eventually, looking straight into his eyes.

"Thank you," James sighs, relieved, "I promise, you won't regret it." He hugs me.

"I probably will," I'm unable to hug him back. "It's ok, you can stay, but you can move into the shed."
"What! The shed?" he looks at me as if he is seeing me for the first time.
"Yes, I don't want you anywhere near me right now," I look back, indigent.
"For how long?"
"Until I can bear to breathe the same air as you again."

After objections, he realises talk is pointless.

James begins to clear out the shed. Old gardening tools and half used tins of paint litter the lawn. We have a blow up camp bed, I don't know why, we never went camping. I see him go red in the face as he uses the foot pump to blow it up. I'm helpful, I find him a duvet and pillows so he's comfortable.

After the first night there are a few moans, his back aches. Good! At the end of his first week there is a bad back, stiff neck and a stubbed toe. Even better! James asks if he can come back in to the house. "Not yet," is the short answer. He asks for the mattress, from the single bed in the small room. Of course, I have no objection, but I don't help him move it.

As James realises it's going to take a bit more remorse, he installs electricity from the main supply in the garage. What follows is a TV from the spare room, a microwave, a kettle and a bench top fridge. Access to the garage which includes a downstairs shower room takes care of his daily ablutions. He's all set.

Over the weeks, the weather turns autumnal. James complains of the cold, hoping I will relent. I won't. I am most helpful again, and I suggest he insulates the shed.

I'm living in comfort, palatial by comparison, but the house is too big for one person. It's a lot of dusting. The estate agent says it will be easy to sell. As I sign the details I'm out of my comfort zone but I remind myself almost anything worth doing in life is accompanied with an element of fear.

Within the week there is a viewing. They don't buy it, but it's encouraging. A couple of months pass in a blur of viewings. There's lots to do; paperwork, certificates and packing.

I'm unsure of myself, shaking, as I arrive to meet with the solicitor to discuss the details of the sale. "And the buyer? He's happy with everything?" I ask.
"Oh yes, he loves the area, great for the schools, for his kids, his wife loves the house, especially the kitchen."
"And with the additional clause in the contract? It's been explained to them?" I look at her out the corner of my eye.
"Yes," she flicks through the papers. "All explained, they're happy. We should complete in a couple of days."

Moving day arrives and I am full of anticipation, regret and excitement. I didn't know it was possible to feel so many emotions at once. The removal men pack up the house, I remind them not to take the cabinet in the hall or anything from the garage. The buyers want the cabinet as part of the deal. I wiz around with a cloth one more time, like the domestic goddess I'm not. I want it to be perfect. After all, we put our heart and soul in to the renovation of this house, our forever home.

Hours later, I sit in my bijou, water front apartment, surrounded by boxes, mountain high. I'm surprised everything went so smoothly, no last minute hitches. I'm more surprised at the new owners, of number 22 Sutton Street, agreeing to my conditions.

It was easy to arrange. Detailing everything in the contract. Registering new boundaries with the Land Registry. The buyers never questioned it. They were just keen to be in the catchment area, so their kids can go to the best high school around for miles.

Selling two thirds of the garden was genius. I still own the garage and the bottom third of the garden. The third of the garden that houses a perfectly good shed and one cheating husband. James will rue the day he asked to put the house into my name, to protect it from his dodgy deals. I can feel my ears burning.

He'll know by now, I smile. Sitting on the balcony, over-looking the river, I raise my prosecco to my lips. I can almost see his face.

I think of the chaos, pure chaos, which reigns at number 22 Sutton Street, in the perfectly good shed, at the bottom of the garden.

Ballad of the Four Houses

Deben, Stour, Waveney, Brett,
The boys from these houses, we chose to forget.
The dark, dank days of Hinklesham Hall
Home for the excluded, with no hope at all.
A colourless, loveless, cold abode;
Anguished and twisted, by something untold.
That boy, some swore, they saw his face.
Others insisted they felt his embrace.
Not a hug with affection, there was no hint of care;
The boys were left gagging and retching, gasping for air.

Deben, Stour, Waveney, Brett,
The boys from these houses, we chose to forget.

Down by the river, the terror was worse.
Water, deep, still and foreboding, black as a hearse.
Swimming was their challenge, all the boys knew the tale
But feared more their penance, should their chapter group fail.
In they would go, young men, trying hard to be brave;
Believing the cane far worse than their grave.

Who would he take next, this boy, this ghoul?
So many, too many boys, lost from this school.
Tangled in debris and reeds, they'd say
But the reality was, deathly hands won the day.
They would grab frantic legs and pull down, far beneath;
Drowning those boys, whom no one would grieve.

Deben, Stour, Waveney, Brett,
The boys from these houses, we chose to forget.

If the Masters knew the truth, then they did not act.
In those days, no questions were ever asked.
The bodies? Some were pulled up, others washed up, miles away on the sand.
Those not so innocent boys, killed by Hell's vengeful hand.
Brett, Waveney, Stour, or Deben.
The boy cared not, which house he'd strike, to get even.

Deben, Stour, Waveney, Brett,
The boys from these houses, we chose to forget.

Long since closed, tall, locked, gates guard the midden.
The story goes that the young, vengeful soul, had never forgiven
The bullies, from each chapter, who abused him and battered
And he took his own life, believing he never mattered.

Deben, Stour, Waveney, Brett,
The boys from these houses, we chose to forget.

One day, the school will reopen, of that I am sure
And the children won't know what there is instore.
That boy will still be there, in that place, so rank;
Waiting, patiently for vengeance, down by the bank.

Deben, Stour, Waveney, Brett.
Remember *that* boy, we chose to forget.

Soulmate

'SUBMIT'

Jenny's heart pounded as she pressed the button. She'd never done anything like this before. She knew plenty of people who did. Online dating was the way to meet new people these days – everyone said so. It didn't take long.

As she checked her profile, she thought she hadn't made too bad a job of it. She'd followed the guidelines; included pictures taken outside and full body shots, pictures showing you doing things with your friends and a write up about your interests that no one reads.

Her nerves kicked in when her phone alerted her to a message. There were quite a few in the first couple of days. Fresh meat, she knew.

By the second week she got a message from Alex. His first introduction was different from all the rest; it was long and asked all kinds of things about her, favourite colour, favourite music etc. It stood out from all the other mundane messages she'd received:

'Hi'

'Hi your pritty'

'Hi what you doing later?????'

The first message from Alex was so well crafted Jenny wondered if he'd been to creative writing classes. He said he was a director of his own company. He was out to impress but she suspected he sent the same message to everyone.

Contact quickly escalated to text messaging. Jenny didn't want to give out her mobile number so she bought a Pay As You Go mobile. Messages from Alex were often, six or seven times a day. He would send her a message late at night, just to say *'Goodnight'*.

Alex was showering her with attention and Jenny was lapping it up. Alex texted, suggested they meet up;

'Would you let me take you out and spoil you on Friday night?'

'How lovely, but I can't make Friday as it's my monthly night out with the girls.' Jenny replied immediately.

‘Saturday night then?’

‘Sorry no, I have a dinner party.’ She messaged back and wished she had such plans.

‘I’m desperate to meet you,’ he typed, ‘I think I’ve met my soulmate.’

After a pause, another message came.

‘How about Sunday lunch?’

‘Yes.’ Jenny’s fingers couldn’t punch the keys fast enough, ‘Sunday would be lovely.

‘Great. I’ll book us a table at Wrexham Hall, they do lovely Sunday lunches.’

Alex was elated when Jenny sent a reply and his phone beeped, ‘Wonderful. I can’t wait.’

While Jenny was out with the girls on Friday night Alex was home alone and couldn’t stop thinking about her. Her long, dark, sultry hair, her wide smile, her perfect white teeth and a body to die for. He couldn’t believe his luck. Intelligent, witty and a fitness instructor! Alex thought all his dreams had come true at once.

He didn’t want to push his luck but he thought about booking a room so they could have some private time,

somewhere to relax and maybe use the spa facilities. So he texted her while she was out.
‘Great idea,’ Jenny returned his message. ‘A swim and a sauna would be wonderful after the week I’ve had.’

Alex was on cloud nine. He was going to see her in her swim suit. Maybe, just maybe, things might develop quicker than he dared to hope. She seemed keen. She always replied to his messages and now she’s agreed to him booking a room.

‘Let me know when it’s booked and the room number, I’ll meet you there.’ she said later that night when he messaged to say goodnight.

Sunday couldn’t come quick enough for both of them.

As Alex opened the door to the room in Wrexham Hall he wasn’t disappointed and he knew Jenny couldn’t fail to be impressed. He was a bit earlier than he told Jenny, as he wanted to make sure everything was perfect. He’d bought her flowers, roses, and perfume. It was expensive, but for Jenny, it was worth every penny if he could see her beautiful, wide smile directed at him.

One o'clock came and went. He'd suggested 1pm so they could have a swim and a sauna, and lunch afterwards - they served until 5pm. Alex checked his watch a million times. He checked his reflection in the mirror almost as much. His hair was spiked with sea salt spray to perfection, no food in his teeth and dressed casually but smart with his new blue shirt and tan boots.

The sun was shining through the window and he could hear the spring song birds singing merrily. He was no expert but he was sure they were calling for their mates; the blue tit, the wren and the robin, they would all be there. He had butterflies.

Then the knock came at the door, 20 minutes late, a women's prerogative. A quick check in the mirror and a spray of breath freshener. He opened the door but instead of finding Jenny, there was a waiter dressed in the usual white shirt and black trousers. A thin man, bearing a silver tray with a bottle of champagne in an ice bucket and chocolates in a white box. Alex stood back to let the waiter enter. He placed the tray on the table.

"I didn't order this?"

“A gift,” the waiter held out his hand for a tip, “I was only asked to deliver it to this room, 507.”
Alex grunted and tipped him, without paying him too much attention. He left the room but Alex was too busy looking at the tray.

He was surprised when his phone bleeped the arrival of a message. It was from Jenny;
‘I’m so sorry sweetheart, I’m unable to make it today. I’ve been called away on business, a conference, and I have to be there for an early morning start tomorrow. I know you will be disappointed. You have gone to such an effort for me and it’s lovely. It’s a long time since anyone did anything so sweet.
Please enjoy your day. I hope the champagne and chocolates help.
I look forward to seeing you on my return.’

Alex threw his phone on the bed and slumped back. He was disappointed, of course he was. He was fed up; the room had cost so much, and to what end? But if it couldn’t be helped. So typical of Jenny, so lovely to think of him and send champagne and chocolates. He mildly berated himself, he should have thought of it.

He popped the cork and poured himself a glass, no point in wasting it. The first mouthful tasted divine and he relaxed. He wasn't a big fan of chocolate but these were dark chocolate truffles. His favourite. How did she know? He couldn't remember telling her but then there'd been so many messages he must have.

Sitting down on the sofa, with the view of the lake and the gardens beyond, he put his feet up with the champagne and chocolates and sent Jenny a text message. He thanked her for the gift and told her how disappointed he was at not meeting her today.

Enjoying the sunshine he waited for Jenny's reply. She must be driving, he consoled himself.

Alex felt tired and his throat was dry. It must be the alcohol. He stood to make a cup of tea and dizzily, he flopped back on to the sofa. His throat constricted. A burning pain racked through his stomach and he shook as a cold sweat swept over him. He doubled over, clutching his guts, but he couldn't stand to go the bathroom. He felt on the sofa for his phone but it was out of reach. His breathing became laboured and he pulled at his collar to try to allow more air to go in. His face drained; it turned grey and his lips went blue.

It was some hours before anyone found him.

The next morning a harsh knock came at Katie's door.
"Mrs Fletcher?" asked one of the police officers.
"Yes," Katie answered in a slow drawl as her eyes narrowed and her brow creased, "What is this about?"
"Can we come in please?"

Once inside the police officers' face dropped, in a practised look of concern.
"Please sit down Mrs Fletcher, we have some bad news for you." Once she sat he continued, "Your husband has been found dead in a room at Wrexham Hall. It seems he may have died sometime last night." he paused to let the information sink in.
"Dead? Are you sure?"
"I'm afraid so."
Katie silently shook her head.
"I'm sorry I know this might be a bit difficult for you but …"
Katie looked at the police officers with wide eyes.

"… We've reason to believe he was to meet a woman called Jenny but we think she may not have arrived. Do you know her?"
Katie let a tear escape.
"Forensics are checking the room now for evidence. Could you come with us please, to identify your husband? Sorry, we're sure it's him but it's a formality."

Katie brushed her fingers through her short blonde hair, wiped at her eyes and searched around the room for her handbag. She stopped to look out of the window. She looked at the lilac tree where the birder feed hung, a blue tit was innocently taking his breakfast. She briefly glanced at the lovely pink fuchsia under the tree with the freshly dug soil, the burial site for her Pay As You Go mobile. Of course, she had used the hoe on the rest of the garden. Only she knew it was freshly dug.

Katie was expecting the police to call but tried not to show it. As she grabbed her coat she told the police officers how she was used to being home alone. Alex was always working late, visiting his mother, or out with the guys. This time he was playing away; *golf* he said it was.

He threatened me again. That was the sleazy arsehole's first mistake. "No more smack for you, not until you've paid up."
I tried to reason with him, to be civil like, "Aw come on! I'm skint man, you know it. I've nothin'," turning out my pockets. I couldn't make it any clearer. "See! Not a fuckin' bean." He shrugged. That pissed me off. "You'll get your bit, you know you will. Soon as I get myself sorted."
"Like shite. I can't tell you how many times I've heard that. Do you think the stuff just grows out of the ground?" He wanted me to beg but he knew there was only two chances of that happening, slim and none.

Drugs are my down fall and I know it; heroin's my weakness. I wish it wasn't. No one knows better than me what levels of depravity I've reached chasing the dragon. Sometimes I hate myself, but I still have some pride.

The room was dark. A shaft of yellow haze cast shadows and gave a glimpse of the warm summer outside. The sheets of plywood didn't quite butt together and left a gap where the sun blasted through the bay window. The heat was stifling. It made the stench worse than usual. I gagged. It stank of piss and sweat and everything in between, including some things I couldn't recognise. Heavily stained mattresses covered the film of filth on the floor boards. I hate this shithole.

"Then no smack for you," he said as he turned his back on me. As if it was that simple. That was his second mistake.

"But I need a fix now, look man, I'm friggin' shaking." I started to feel the pain and sweat ran down my back. My throat was dry and my head felt like daggers digging in deeply. I had to get a fix, and quick.

"You'll have to pay like anyone else in your position then, won't you? No more freebies." As he turned around he started to undo his flies. "On your knees then – you're a big boy now. A bit too big actually, but you'll do. I'm looking forward to this, being banged up must have taught you a few tricks."

He reached forward with his filthy, fat fingers and dirty nails. Digging in to my flesh he pushed me to my knees by my shoulders. I resisted at first but he had his weight behind him. My knees caved and I went down. Pain shot through my leg as a nail sticking out of the floorboard pierced under my knee. I ignored it. He forced my head towards his crotch. Instead of pulling back, like I've done before, I went with it. I knew it was pointless to resist.

The pungent stench of stale urine mixed with old spunk made me want to heave. Vomit stuck in my throat and I held the heel of my hand tight to my mouth to stop it spewing out. Pale yellow stains lodged in the creases in his jeans, where the blue was worn away. He looked, and smelt, like he'd pissed himself, more than once. Filthy, dirty sod.
"It's taken me a while to break you in laddie. I hope it's going to be worth it." He sneered as his grip around the back of my head tightened.

As he pulled his tiny sweaty dick from his manky pants, I nearly laughed. It was stubby and fat. The end while hard looked like an onion. I tilted my head down towards him. "That's it lad. Give it a good go. Suck hard." His anticipation heightened.

With the top of my head I smacked in to his swollen cock. He screamed, startled and the fuckwit swore but I saw the shock on his face. The whites of his eyes glowed in the dark, dingy hole, when I knocked him off his feet. What did he expect for fuck's sake? What did he think I'd been inside for?

It happened so fast but I felt like I was watching in slow motion. I'm not sure he would agree.

I heard his head crack as it smashed open on the old fireplace. Blood sprayed as he went down and hit the floor with a thud. I think he was dead before he reached the dirty, greasy teal blue rug in front of the fire. A pool of blood spilled out around his head, turning the blue black where the sticky mess soaked in.

He looked older with the colour drained from his face. He was pathetic, with his limp dick flopping out from his zip.

I looked around and there were a couple of geezers lying strung out, twatted, on the mattresses. A pool of dried puke on the floor boards next to one of them and drool hung out of his mouth. I looked at the other, his eyes rolled back as his head flopped to one side. They were fucked up alright. I could have pulled a gun and shot them all in the head, quite fucking easily, and they wouldn't have had a clue. They were that shitfaced.

I helped myself to the tossa's stash, and as much cash as I could find lying about the place. Then I done a runner, didn't I? I might have nowhere to go but didn't want to be found high in that shithole; not with those losers and an old paedo.

The last nonce who tried that game with me got the same, 'cept I didn't kill him. That's where I went wrong. They never learn, no one threatens me and I'm no one's fucking bitch.

Section 3.14

The stress in the office on Court day is palpable, so if I'm not on duty, I take flexi on Wednesdays and never get to my desk before 9.30am. I arrived at 10am, this particular Wednesday. Meg had already left for Court, so no close encounters in the corridor with her; checking who is where, doing what. The 'hall prefect' Darren called her. We all agreed.

Darren joined our team about two months earlier and was still on probation. Ex-military he reckoned. I thought Police, because he drove a Focus but he said he used to guard the Queen from a sentry box at Windsor. He couldn't have been in the Army very long, as he was only 23; clearly there was a story there but I wasn't going to highlight it. He said he didn't like teenagers but the Council's pension was a 'no brainer' after leaving the Army so ...

Katie sits opposite me. Fairy Princess I call her, as she has this 'I'm a spoilt brat, I love myself and every man should fall at my feet' thing about her. Darren did just that, despite having a girlfriend. Apart from being too confident in his ability and getting paid far too much for having half a degree in something microbiological, which is totally irrelevant for this job, I found his mouth was the wrong shape for his face and he was hard to look at. He also made no qualms about hating cats and would talk about the various ways he would torture them if he could. Fairy Princess said he was similar to Brad Pitt but I couldn't see it. He couldn't have been over 5ft 4, he had the makings of a beer belly and receding black curly hair. Perhaps there was a more tenuous link; perhaps his girlfriend was called *Angelina.*

Not much work happens in the office on a Wednesday. Meg is out of the way all day and the week's reports have been done. Even though we each have, seven or eight new ones on our desks to complete for next week's Court date, we consider Wednesday a day of rest.

I came into work to find that, as usual, one of the reports I had prepared for Court that day, had only been printed off moments before it was due. That meant Meg hadn't had a chance to review my pre-sentence conclusions prior to the Magistrates reading the report for the 15 year old, experienced, shop lifter.

Meg wouldn't be worried and nor was I. My reports were always commended by the magistrates for being well written and not ambiguous, unlike some I could mention.

When I plonked myself at my desk, I noted that Fairy Princess was leaning over Darren, smelling of Jimmy Choo and watching something on YouTube. I think it was a clip from one of those *The Real Housewives of* wherever shows, these youngsters like. Her eyes were glued to his PC screen and his nose was practically wedged in her cleavage. I find this type of behaviour horribly fascinating; a bit like watching a wildlife programme where the male, of some exotic insect species, gets devoured by the female, in broad daylight. Oh they do make me chuckle.

I had just returned from the tea room. I am being generous calling it that, as it's a stationery cupboard next to the toilets with the drain issue. I always go to the loos downstairs but sadly, the others don't, so the cupboard is the collection point for various rotten egg smells with a hint of bleach. It does house the only kettle and microwave in the building. Although the kettle has metamorphosed into lime scale with a plug and you don't want to start me on the microwave! I am the only one that cleans it, yet every lunch time, without fail, I open the door to pop in something home-made, only to be greeted by nothing short of the Muppet Show; there are so many living organisms inside. The Fairy Princess says that's why she doesn't eat. Hygiene issues in the workplace she says. I say eating disorder but what do I know?

I put the hot mugs down, loudly, on my desk for them to help themselves. I'm not a waitress. Fairy Princess and Darren had moved on from YouTube and were checking out the online cocktail menu for Wincy's; the new place we all go to for special work nights out. They were planning to go that Friday. Darren would tell his girlfriend it was a leaving do. We've had more leaving dos than staff who have ever worked here but that was his business, I couldn't possibly comment.

Fairy Princess said Meg had been on and wanted me to ring her back urgently and she was 'stressy' about something. When was she not? Being exceptionally efficient, I rang the Court immediately. I didn't think much of it, as the legal teams sometimes want clarification about something in the report but mine are very clear so I doubted that was it.

Well, she came on the phone and I could hear something strange in her voice, like she was going to cry, which is unheard of, so I put it down to giddiness. Meg loves Wednesdays at Court, especially when she gets the results she wants. So, she told me, in a hushed, wobbly little voice, that there was something wrong with my report. *My* report! That's all she said, without any expansion for a full 30 seconds! So, in my firm voice – someone had to be in control - I asked her what she meant. She said the Magistrates had pointed out an 'anomaly' and the defence solicitor was apoplectic about a few sentences in section 3.14. Apparently they all knew before she did and she felt ridiculous. So, it was about her.

She was rambling on. I switched off. I thought she'd had caffeine; she was breathy, like her heart was beating too fast. She sounded like my friend Margaret after she's eaten too many cola cubes. I wondered if all those late nights at work had finally twisted that madness key in Meg's brain. We all heard her talking and laughing out loud to herself when we mass exodus past her office at 5.30pm. Kev, from Reparation lives on Chatterton Terrace, two minutes down the road from work. He walks his dog past here, after 11pm most nights. He has to, or his dog will mess in the house. He said the lights are always on upstairs, when he walks past. He never alerts anyone of course, as he knows it's her. We all know Meg's here more hours than she is at home.

'*Deborah*' she said, not Debs, as I'm known by her and everyone else; clearly she wanted to make a point. What had I been thinking when I wrote section 3.14, she had asked accusingly? Before I could say anything she enquired had I not attended the prosocial behaviour training in March? Well she knew I had, because Sandra from Admin had one of her nose bleeds and Meg had asked me to see if I could get some toilet roll. Neil, from Interventions, had got Sandra a serviette, thinking it to be more absorbent than tissue paper but it was made from that shiny, viscose material and was no use at all.

I responded that she knew I had! I also reminded her that I am aware 3.14 is a very important section in the report about the young person's education, employment and training and any income deriving from such! I heard a bit of a whimper when I said that and she immediately asked if I wouldn't mind opening up the report on my PC, because it would be easier if I took a look rather than her explaining.

What she actually said was "Will you just stop talking and bring up the fucking report on your PC screen!"

Knowing one has to tread very carefully when someone's mind has snapped, I thought it pertinent to comply; best to humour her and calm the situation, than risk her becoming homicidal in the Court's canteen, if someone didn't pass the tomato sauce. I couldn't be responsible for that.

Darren and the Fairy Princess had cottoned on that something was not quite the norm and they appeared either side of me, like mismatched bookends, just as my report popped up on screen. I scrolled down to the paragraph in question. Well, I'm not sure who spotted it first, me, the Princess, or Darren. I have to say the paragraph flowed well with the rest of my report. Yes, the teen did have a hygiene problem and yes, pretty much everything that came out of his mouth had been bullshit. That's BULLSHIT in capital letters, your Worships but *I* didn't write that! I gasped when I read the inclusion of those alien sentences for the first time. Meg hadn't finally flipped. Her marbles were intact. Section 3.14 was far from Court room appropriate and, it was a big problem!

There was another whimper on the other end of the telephone when I told her I had read it and I hadn't known anything about it. From a legal point of view, I could hear how defenceless that sounded. I made some sort of unintelligible noise back at Meg. I saw Fairy Princess put her hand to her mouth in shock, at the same time Darren's face turned alabaster white and he began to back away from the computer, saying something out loud, that I am sure he thought he'd said in his head. I will never forget that moment, the nail in the coffin moment for Darren. He said, "Bu… but, I deleted that!"

And there it was. Darren had decided it would be funny, at an opportune moment, when I was in the stationery cupboard, no doubt, to spice up the report I'd been working on. I think he was showing off to the Fairy Princess, who probably egged him on with her stuck on eyelashes and long, wafty hair. He claimed that it most certainly was his intention to delete it after I had read it. He said he must have been distracted with a call or such like - the Fairy Princess more like – and he had completely forgotten about it. The offensive paragraph had remained in Section 3.14 for the Magistrates to ponder on. The thing is, I should have read though my report but I hadn't.

I was reprimanded that very afternoon for failing to check my report, before it went to Court and for leaving the room without locking my computer - which was a bit rich, in my opinion, as everyone did it. I was so upset, I had to go home for the rest of the day, and lie down. The injustice! Meg said the warning will stay on my record for 6 months. Months! I didn't stop crying until Coronation Street and even then, I wasn't in the right frame of mind to take it all in. Darren only wrote what we had all been thinking. I planned to tell them all that.

The next morning, before I had a chance to say anything, I found that Meg and her Manager, Andrew, did not think working for the Youth Offending Team was *for* Darren and his probation period was terminated with immediate effect.

I learned that Darren had hot-footed it to the Court when he'd heard I left distressed yesterday. He had apologised profusely to the Magistrates and the family of the young offender. He had also made it very clear that, although my name was on the report, it had nothing to do with me. I have to remind myself of his views about cats and his poor unknowing girlfriend. Still …

Darren left us that day, to do something more microbiological he said, but we all knew he'd been given the heave-hoe. No one went to Wincy's after work; not even the Fairy Princess. I think he thought he would be more popular. Too short notice for me, I have Mr Puss to consider.

The Fairy Princess now has eyes for Darren's replacement, Laurence, who was parachuted in from another youth offending team. They wanted someone who knew the ropes. Time will tell with his report writing skills but he makes a grand cuppa and has no time for her, whatsoever. He told me he has three cats.

Perfect Chance

It's a busy street in the centre of town, the hustle and bustle is entrancing, full to the brim with people of all colours and all cultures. Everyone who lives there, and is out and about at this time, is making their way to work with their heads full; lost in their own thoughts and wrapped up in themselves. Those that don't belong, are tourists mainly, excitedly chatting to each other, with or without maps, planning their day. The pavement is awash with bobbing heads.

While waiting for the lights to change and the green man to illuminate, to indicate it's safe to cross, I gently nudge forward and the man at the front of the crowd is pushed off the curb.

No one notices the push.

The car screeches. I'm too far back to see it, but the smell of burning brake fluid and melting rubber explodes heavily into the air. As the un-mistakable thud of a limp body hits the bonnet, universal gasps erupt.

My plan was only to help him twist his ankle, a sprain would do it, at most a break, not kill the man outright. He’s done nothing to deserve it.

Some people move away in the opposite direction, they don’t want their day ruined with witness statements. Some people rush forward to get a better look. Some people have their mobile phone cameras poised. It will be viral in moments.

I join those going in the opposite direction, dragging my legs which are made of lead. My head pounds. I’m spurred on by my racing heart. Thumping. Mechanical. A vivid image spinning through my mind; his body spinning in the air then lying still, unmoving, and single trickle of blood seeping from his ear.

It takes two days to receive the phone call I expect.

“Would you mind? Are you free? Please, please, we need you?”
I don’t answer; there’s a pause … an uncomfortable silence.
“We wouldn’t ask but we’ve been let down …”

I hold my breath and I'm not forthcoming. More silence. I'm second best.
"He's not answering his phone, or returning our calls…"
The quiet is deafening.
"… And no one else is available …" she sighs.

Now, I'm third, or is that fourth, fifth, or sixth best? How many others did she try before getting round to asking me?
"I know it's very short notice … but please, we don't know what else to do. Please would you take our photographs on our wedding day?"
"Of course," I eventually let her off the hook. "Anything for you."

Plans had stretched before us from a very young age, at the first sight of a bride. We were both mesmerised; the beautiful white dress and the long train held in her arms, so it wouldn't get dirty. Her face masked by the white veil, with little daisies embroidered on it. Her smile radiated and refused to be hidden. She stepped, right foot first, out of the house into the bright sunlight; she looked like an angel. With his hand outstretched in the door way, she was helped down the step by her proud father, in his slivery grey top hat and tails. It was like a dream, right down to the fancy cream car, with a silver lady standing to attention at the front. And, of course, white ribbons tied across the bonnet to the wing mirrors, flapping in the gentle breeze.

The excitement grew as we joined the other children in the wedding scramble; collecting as many of the coins as we could, thrown down by the father of the bride at the 'toss out'. Two grubby girls, side by side, elbows at the ready.

Long summers were spent with every Saturday sitting on the dry stone wall surrounding the little church. Waiting for a glimpse of white, waiting for a glimpse of our future. Promises were made to each other. Head bridesmaids, both of us for each other, best friends forever, while linking our little fingers of our right hands. A pact. A pinky promise.

Our dresses were designed, every detail planned – our special day would not be left to chance. Of course the dress design was revised over the years, as styles

changed and girls grew, but one thing always remained the same, we were always together.
"I won't let you down. What are best friends for?" The phone is hot in my hand.
I can feel the relief in her *thank you.*

Her wedding is perfect, just as we'd planned it. All except for one teensy, weensy, little detail; the head bridesmaid.

I snap all day long. Covering every angle, every expression, and every guest. I leave nothing, or no one, out.

She'd met her man, 'the one' she told me. She couldn't wait to divulge every little detail, relishing and reliving every moment. I relived them with her. Lying on my sofa, with a bottle of wine and pizza, she told me everything, down to his perfect little creases and his cute dimples every time he laughed.

As time progressed, she moved on, she made new friends - couples. I became surplus to requirements, I guess. I saw her less and less. I wasn't invited on nights out anymore. I wasn't invited to the hen do. My invitation to the wedding must have been lost in the post.

As their big day draws to a close, they flit off on their honeymoon. I'm left to pack away my kit into my car on my own. Not even a glass of champagne for me. All work.

I'm pleased with the shots, they've printed up well. I take my time and I carefully select the photographs I want to deliver to them on their return. I pick just fifteen photographs, fifteen of the best. Enough, I reckon, to do the job I'm paid for. The other pictures I present to the bride and groom are … well, let's just say, the happy couple are less than happy. I bet they wish they hadn't asked me to take their pictures when their first choice of photographer was tragically run over.

Rows, threats and a summons leads to a court case. I'm only a student, 'the risks were all theirs,' the Judge rules, 'there's no contract and they shouldn't have left their *special day* to chance. It's their own fault'.

Returning to my flat, I'm constantly surprised by the skill I've demonstrated, the expertise. It's a good college course and I've come a long way in such a short time. I step back to admire my handiwork, with a sense of pride. Perfect. I congratulate myself. People would pay good money for shots like these.

More than three hundred photographs completely covers my sitting room wall and each one is different; colour, sepia, black and white, coloured filters. All in focus, all different angles, all different shots, but for one teensy, weensy little detail; from each one, looking back at me, is the face of my best friend and the lucky man, her husband, on their special day.

I look at the photographs and I decide on the one. Not the best, not the second best, not even the third, fourth, or fifth best. I finally settle on the sixth best. I choose the one I wish to send them as a gift for their first anniversary, paper. It couldn't be more perfect.

There's something about Christmas ...

"Gary, there's something about Christmas I can only liken to childbirth." He didn't ask me to explain but I did anyway. Henry was busy on his iPad game and Anna was watching a DVD on the portable. Both head-phoned and on a different plane to the rest of humanity! We had been crawling along the M1 for hours. Something about being in cars helps me formulate my thoughts.

"We have all the build-up for months before the due date, we attend all the things we need to; school nativities, Christmas markets, church services, and school fayres. We do all this to ensure we are as prepped as we can be for the big day. We shop endlessly and, on that subject, you know Maureen, who bought her third freezer just for Christmas food, last year? Well she told Karen, who told me at Olivia's on Friday night, that she bought her forth last week, in a pre-Christmas clear out, 30% off sale!"

Gary looked at me in a questioning way, his left eyebrow became animated for a split second; my cue to continue - with more detail. He would want to know what on earth she kept in freezers one, two and three to warrant such a necessity!

"She has her day to day, frozen foods in her main fridge freezer – her nice black one with the ice dispenser? And she keeps her home-made desserts and party, frozen fancies in the second one, you know, those nice gateaux tartlets you rave about at the Rotary and the mini cheesecakes and crumbles she brings to the PTA and Rugby dos?"

Gary clearly wanted to know more about my childbirth and Christmas comparison, as he asked me what my point was. He sounded weary, the slow moving traffic clearly getting to him. Does like to put his foot down does Gary! That's why we sold the old 4X4 and we now drive this sporty hatch back. I say, *we,* but I rarely drive these days. Not after the bollard incident outside the school. I forgot the new car has a longer front to the old one. Gary got front parking sensors fitted when the car got fixed but I still don't feel comfortable in the driver's seat. Gary said I should get back into driving as soon as possible, especially as he needs me to pick him up from the pub after football practise on a Sunday. I don't know, the whole thing shook me up. Not just denting the bumper which, incidentally, cost an arm and a leg to fix but no … the dog! I mean, who the hell would tie a dog to a bollard, for crying out loud!

"Anyway, childbirth and Christmas …" I continued, as I could tell Gary was desperate to hear more. He gesticulated a forward winding motion, with his gear stick hand; his eyes unmoved from the rear bumper of the car in front of us.

"We have certain expectations for the big day. The worry too; will it all go to plan? Will everything be ok? Then, the day itself comes and we are usually already exhausted by then and just need to get through it. After all, It's hard work; late night shopping, trying to find the perfect gifts, swollen ankles from all the walking and then lugging the bags of shopping home. And the wrapping, the endless wrapping; tying bows, sticking on labels and writing cards out to people we don't speak to from one year to the next.

Then, the 'joys' of the food preparation that only wine can get me through. The stress and hours of labour in the kitchen; the toing and froing of people, having to be ushered out with promises they'll be called if needed. I always get to the point where I feel I just can't physically do it - twelve pans of veg on a 4 ringed hob? I mean it is nigh on impossible! And all the sweating over timings … don't start me on the fluid loss!

But we convince ourselves it's all worth it, for that moment, *the* moment, when the turkey can be seen to be browning and we know we only have minutes to wait. Then finally, the sheer exultation when it's lifted out, for the world to see; gasps of relief and joy at its safe delivery to the dining room, where family and loved ones have congregated in anticipation." Gary sighed which I took as empathy, so I carried on.

"Everyone from each side of the family toasts each other, like *they* have done something amazing. They're generous and cordial with one another, until the fourth glass of wine is imbibed. Then, tensions start to build and an atmosphere fills the room and I just want them all to fuck off, so I can enjoy the bloody turkey!" Gary asked if I was finished. I said nearly.

"On Christmas day, the children are knackered, having been up since sunrise. Everyone becomes overwrought with emotion. My sister starts *remember whening* and my mother falsely reminisces about my drunken, abusive father, who died eleven years ago!" I quickly check the back seat, to make sure the children didn't hear that part. They hadn't. So immersed in their electronic devises, I doubt they would have noticed if their dad and me got beamed out of the car by aliens.

Gary looked like he was about to speak but I quickly jumped in. I needed to finish my point, or I'd have lost my thread.

"Then it's tidy up time; a bit like the reaction you get when changing that very first, full nappy. Predictably, some people go home then, or at the very least, leave the room to sit in front of the telly to watch something they have, *apparently,* waited for all Christmas. Others loiter and pick at the stray pieces of Christmas cake, looking awkward, as if they know they could be helpful but don't really want to be.

Drunken conversations continue and start to make no bloody sense and I just want to go to sleep, knowing the next day will be just as busy, with visitors coming and going. It's all just so draining! Yet, we do it again and again, because we forget all the bad bits; all the pain and tiredness, the worry and sleepless nights. Just so we can have this one, bloody, day a year!"

Gary reminded me that at least I wasn't the one cooking this year, hence the long journey to *his* mother's. When Gary realised I had finished my postulations, he turned the radio up from the little buttons on the steering wheel. I pressed the horn, when I tried to do it in the showroom. Michael Bublé's new festive, chart climber filled the car. I love Michael.

The car stopped completely. Little wispy, white feathers floated down onto the gridlocked traffic. I felt all overcome with the romance of the moment and touched Gary's knee.

Gary switched to another station; that was the end of Michael. He then blurted out that he had been seeing someone else for the last ten months. He didn't take his eyes off the road, despite our static condition. He said this would be our last Christmas together. I looked round to the back seat and the children were still plugged in. They didn't have a clue the world had just ended.

"This Christmas won't be like childbirth at all then …" I wobbled out my words and removed my hand.

Henry

Oh God Almighty, not again! How the hell did this happen? His head spins with sickening panic.

He's cold, *damn it*, and tired with an overwhelming, and all too familiar, feeling of self-loathing. And he can't remember a thing.

Henry lifts his head from the damp mound of moss he's using for a pillow. He can taste the morning dew, sweet, fresh moisture envelops his lips and nostrils. Mist glistening like pale custard in the yellow glow of the nearby light, which is yet to extinguish.

He wakes unusually early and a chill permeates through his bones. He has a fearsome pain in his head and a stiff neck. Every muscle in his body aches. He's acutely aware of the first stirrings of people going about their normal, daily routine, noisily. Every sound, every step crunching on the gravel, feels like an ice pick slamming into his head. Each gentle tweet of a bird is a pneumatic drill.

Completely dishevelled, Henry runs his hands through his lank, matted hair and scratches. He rubs the sand paper stubble on his chin and tries to remember the last time he shaved, but the answer escapes him. A faint acidic smell of fresh urine, mingles with stale sweat and assaults his nose. He pulls his old, comfortable jacket around his meaty shoulders in a bid to shield himself from the cold as he lies on the ground.

His head banging, his body aching all over and his throat as dry as the Sahara, gives Henry the motivation to prise his cumbersome, frame off the ground. Lifting himself slowly he staggers to his feet and begins to walk, gingerly. The sound and pressure of his footfall smacks into his head with every step.

Henry makes his way home, to his nice, warm house where there will be the smell of bacon cooking on the stove. He salivates as he can almost taste it, the crispy bacon, the melting butter and, his favourite, cold tomato sauce - straight from the fridge. His mother will be in her apron, standing in front of the cooker. He knows, as he enters the kitchen, she will frantically wave the spatula at him, as she playfully tells him off.

She will act annoyed, they both know she isn't, but they go through the pretence all the same. She'll laugh, with that infectious giggle of hers, which he never gets sick of hearing.

As he walks up the garden path he gets a dreadful feeling, the house is in darkness. Total darkness. Henry stops to check his watch, maybe it's earlier than he thinks, but it isn't. Maybe his mother has overslept, but that's isn't like her at all. Not at all. Something is definitely wrong and he knows it.

Turning the lock, slowly with trepidation, he pushes the door open. He notices the blue paint work flaking as it crackles beneath his fingers and shards drop to the ground. The step has a light film of bright green slime. The garden is over grown. Henry doesn't understand it, he trimmed the hedges back, just last week, hadn't he? It's all a bit fuzzy.

Henry pushes the door open and hears a creek of dry hinges, that wasn't there before, he's sure of that. He would need to oil them later. There are no lights on, no warmth and no bacon cooking. Just gloom and the musty smell of damp. Wallpaper is peeling at thc corners and the carpet is so threadbare in the hall, he can feel the floorboards beneath his heavy, leather biker boots.

Feeling nauseous, his heart beats heavily and his already thumping head begins to throb, unbearably. There's something he needs to remember but he can't quite grasp it. Something important.

Quietly, his mother appears in the doorway, she looks older, her hair's tinged with grey not the usual dark brown locks she was so proud of. As expected, she's wearing one of her many dresses with her apron over the top. But Henry notices she's looking pale and anxious, as she wrings her apron in her hands.

"Where have you been all day Henry, my precious son? I've been worried." The worry's evident, she speaks with a shaky voice. He suspects she's close to tears, but she will never allow him to see her cry.

"In the Churchyard my dear mother. Please help me, please make my bed. I have pains in my head and I really need to go to sleep." The look of despair crosses his mothers' face, but only for a fleeting second, it's barely noticeable really, but Henry sees it.

Soundlessly, and without a single word of reprisal, his mother makes her way up the stairs. Mounting one step at a time, her legs only just manage to carry her. Henry follows, close on her heals. Taking fresh linen from the cupboard she expertly makes up his bed, as she has done many times before. Henry wastes no time and slides under the covers. He isn't in bed long enough to smell the fresh sheets, feel the warmth of the blankets or the softness of the pillow. He feels safe, secure and sleep takes over.

Henry wakes the next morning, freezing cold, with the same excruciating pains in his head. He shivers as the wind whistles around him. Henry's mind is fog and he can't remember … anything.

He opens his eyes, a few minutes before lifting his head, feeling sick to his stomach, tired and in desperate pain. His head thumps and feels like a lead weight on top of his neck. He touches the cold glass of an empty vodka bottle lying next to him. He lifts his head tentatively, craning his neck to look around; slowly, he raises himself on to one elbow. The wet grass seeps through the arm of his jacket. Henry looks above his head and jolts as he sees a headstone for the first time. Adjusting his eyes to focus on the engraved inscription.

Here lies Henry James
Tragically, taken too soon
Age 24

His breath falters in his throat, bile rises, he leans forward, retching, vomiting. His heart pounds and he shakes. There's a lump of coal in his chest. Henry's in shock; his temples beat fast and he feels numb. He continued reading.

Sylvia James
Aged 62.
Beloved mother of the late Henry James
Simply past with a broken heart
Will be sadly missed

Henry bows his head. His throat constricts as he tries to hold back his tears; he can't. One big, fat tear slides down his cheek, streaking though the dirt on his face and dropping from his chin onto the grass. He gives way and allows himself to sob. The pain in his head magnifies. He shakes uncontrollably as the memories come flooding back.

He remembers feeling the heat from the sun as the warm air rushes through the bandana across his face. He can smell freshly cut grass, spring time; everything is new and alive. He's full of hope for the summer to come. A fly hits his sun glasses and splats blood in front of his left eye, the inconvenience, irritated, he would have to stop now and clean his glasses.

Vivid images all come rushing in one almighty sprint. The dip in the road, with the puddle left by the spring shower he's just missed. If he'd been ten minutes earlier he would have had a real soaking. He's counts himself lucky.

The road rushing up to meet him, as his motorbike skids to the right; the smell of burning rubber and the sound of metal scraping. Adrenalin coursing through Henry's body as his crash helmet hits the ground, seconds before his motorbike lands on top of him. His head bouncing and he feels the instant, excruciating pain as his face smashes into the dark, grey, tarmac – then – nothing!

He isn't there to feel the warm rush of blood from under his helmet, to see the dark red sticky stain spread across the road, or to hear his mother's constant cries, night after night, into her damp pillow. It's just black, soundless, oblivion. Henry is gone.

Inspired by a well know folk song of which there are many versions worldwide.

Where have you been all day Henry my son?
Where have you been all day my blessed one?
In the Churchyard dear mother, Churchyard dear mother
Oh please make my bed for there's pains in my head and I want to go to sleep.

Sea Air

If I were blindfolded, I would know exactly where I was. The muffled conversations of so many families and the young and the old, enjoying the late summer sun; the squeals of happy children; the occasional playful dog barking and the smells … aah, the smells alone conjure up a whole film reel of pictures, so vivid, I don't need eyes.

I feel a light breeze skim my hair and with it wafts over one of the nation's favourite aromas. I can never decide whether I prefer this mouth-watering scent of fish and chips to freshly baked bread, or a bacon sandwich. For all of which, I firmly hold that the anticipation of that first bite far exceeds the reality of the taste. Yet, I know I will buy a portion of chips before I head home and they will be smothered to death with salt and drowned in gallons of vinegar. They don't stand a chance!

I have barely exhaled away that intoxicating smell before something sickly sweet fills my airways. Like a Siren's song, I am drawn to the sign which reads '£4 for 10 small donuts'. I can imagine the sugar in my mouth and my tongue reacts, skimming my lips but all I can taste is a light layer of salt from the sea air. I think of the chips I plan to have after my stroll and have to swallow away the excess saliva my taste buds have spontaneously produced. I'm not even hungry. Those heavenly, seaside food smells are tempting me. I have no willpower.

As I walk onto the sand, the breeze gifts me with a more natural odour from the sea. Seaweed lies in clumps along my path. It's strong in the heat; the smell catches me off guard; really strong, sweaty fish in the midday heat. I wrinkle my nose and breath more shallowly, walking onward.

The stale sea air is getting stronger and to top it, a sulphuric stench now dances about with it, in the light wind. A young family of four, squashed onto a beach towel, are eating egg sandwiches. They were bound up in cling film for too long I decide. They smell warm. I turn away remembering my childhood and of hard boiled eggs, unleashed from foil, on our 'whatever the weather' family picnics.

The seaweed has become rancid, overpowering, as I walk on towards the shore. I'm seriously questioning my want for chips now.

Muffled conversations and light chatter grows louder - shouty and the squeals of the children aren't as joyous as they were. They are not playing anymore. A few children are screaming and I can hear cries. The playful occasional barking is now frantic and relentless. People are gathering, surging almost, to the water's edge. A man in a baseball cap rushes past me, cheeks bulging, lips greasy wet; clinging onto his polystyrene tray, overflowing with battered cod and thick soggy chips that I know will be vinegar sodden and crystallised with salt. All I can smell is something sour. Rotten. Unappetising.

Children are pulled away from the surf and taken away from the beach entirely; others are pushed forward by eager parents, desperate to see what is causing such fascination.

"Is that a big fishy?" a small boy asks.

"I can't see, lift me!" another demands.

"It's just an upturned boat," a woman dismisses. She pulls her charge away in haste, acting like it is far from just an ‘upturned boat.’ Others, faces blanched, follow and begin pushing back up towards through the hordes of shorts and tee-shirts, which are immovable and still trying to get a glimpse of whatever it is.

Intrigued now, I want to go and take a look myself but before I get much further, a pungent, eye watering, stench of ammonia and dead flesh, hits the back of my throat. I think I will vomit as my stomach lurches but I don’t quite gag. Breathing deeply, I know I’m definitely not having chips on the way back. The baseball hat has stopped eating from his tray of golden delight. Not even the gods’ own cuisine can mask this revolting attack on the senses.

“Oh God there are so many!” A woman just in front of me sounds like she’s about to cry. I edge myself forward.

I don’t need to look at the decaying bodies of those who sought refuge in a foreign land. I don’t need to hinder the help of so many, pulling the drowned women and children to the sand they never got to feel between their toes. I don’t need to go to the water’s edge to witness their bloated and rotting shells to feel angry and helpless.

I don’t need to see any of it, the sea air is enough.

Leather versus Rubber

The water gently swills over the top of the causeway. At first, it's quite pretty with small fish skimming the concrete path. Maggie panics of course. She's wearing her new shoes. I told her earlier, "Maggie, you better put your trainers on, those rocks can be slippery."
She says, "I might as well put my wellies on then."
We laughed at that, the thought of Maggie in wellies.
"Besides," she says, "my trainers haven't been worn yet and I don't want to get them dirty."
I'm astounded. "Not worn yet?" I ask her. "You've been going to the gym for 6 weeks now. How are they not worn?"
"Oh, I don't do anything. I'm just at the watching stage. I'm not sure about getting all sweaty. That's not for me." It seems Maggie's dainty little dancers have never been anywhere near a flat pair of shoes.

I'm all ready to stride across the causeway and be damned, but Maggie chooses this moment to have one of her cramps, and I know what that means. There's no moving her.

We’re standing on St Mary’s Island, on the rocks below the bank, looking at the causeway, which is disappearing rapidly under water. Well, I’m standing. Maggie is doubled over. I try to put my arm around her to help, to be supportive, but I’m met with an icy stare. A look colder than the North Sea, which, incidentally, is starting to get a little bit naughty.

I take my shoes and socks off and start rolling up my trouser legs. Even doubled over Maggie still manages the energy to bark at me.

“What are you doing, Jim?”

“I’m about to be your hero, you know, like I used to be. I’m heading over to the car to get help.”

“What? In your bare feet?”

“I don’t want to ruin my new shoes. We bought them specially.”

“Oh,” says Maggie pointing at my feet disgruntled, “What do you think you have there, then? Flippers?” She can be funny at times but I don’t think that’s her real laugh. It’s a bit strangled, like seagulls squawking for food. I look at her with concern but she doesn’t waiver.

A discussion follows, in rather a lot of detail, about the merits of leather soles versus rubber soles. Maggie's in favour of leather. My explanation of the superior grip you get with rubber soles falls on deaf ears. "I read it in a magazine," I tell her, but it has no impact. Even though she's wearing leather, I decide to leave that particular line of conversation and refocus on the task at hand, or should I say foot.

I turn back to the rising tide which is coming in quickly. The sea is covering the causeway and has cut us off completely. Black clouds linger over head, threatening. The sea is ferocious, crashing and banging on the rocks, splashing spray indiscriminately. I'm a little bit scared but try not to show it.

Maggie, unaware of the encroaching North Sea, is more bothered about sand in her toes. I tell her, "It will be more than sand soon enough, if you don't watch your step." It's as if I conjure it up, a big wave crashes up against the entire Island and completely engulfs us. Maggie jumps bolt upright and screeches like a banshee, her cramps completely forgotten.

"No need to worry about my new leather shoes getting wet," as I look at the empty space they occupied. "They're gone!"
"For God's sake," Maggie says, "Is that all you can talk about, at a time like this, while we are stranded, you're flaming leather shoes?"
"Well," I say, feeling put out. "What would you like me to talk about? Lipstick?"
Then she says, "You probably know all about those as well, do you?"
I look at her in her new soggy, sandals. Her hair is matted and mascara is streaking down her face. She looks like she is going to cry. I feel sorry for her but I don't know what she wants me to say. So I say, "Well..."

Maggie turns a funny colour, not her usual orangey colour at all. She huffs a couple of times and I think she's gasping for air, like a fish, and then she just comes out with it. "That's it. Why we couldn't go to Prague or Rome for the weekend, like everyone else, I don't know."

Maggie and I came to Whitley Bay for a long weekend and I couldn't resist going to St. Mary's Island for a walk on a romantic moonlit night.

She's almost screaming now, "That is it. I WANT A DIVORCE!"
"Calm down Maggie, you're just upset because your new shoes are wet. I told you to put your trainers on."
Except she's not laughing this time. I don't know how to cheer her up anymore.
"You really have been a rubbish husband."
I'm not sure what she means. I've done all my jobs.
"I only married you to get away from my mother!"
That cut me. I know she hates her mother. All I do is look at her with her pink lipstick smudged around her mouth, which is exaggerating her grimace.

A wave, as strong as a ten pound hammer, hits my calves. I rock forward, knees bending with the force. I see the heel of Maggie's shoe buckle as it twists her foot inwards. She begins to topple. She swings her arms to steady herself. "Do something, you useless Oaf," she spits.

In that split second our eyes lock in comprehension. It could have gone either way. I reach out to grab her but find it only takes one gentle shove. She bounces off the rocks and is pulled down in to the water in no time.

As the tide washes Maggie away the last thing to go under is her feet, in her new leather sandals. I think she would be happy with that but I still can't help thinking she would have been better off wearing her trainers.

I retreat to higher ground. I'm wet enough. To sit with my back against the lighthouse I take off my rucksack. I know Maggie hated it, she never missed on opportunity to tell me I looked like a nerd but I think it's rather smart and handy.

I open my flask of soup and eat my meat paste sandwiches. I take in the view, it really is spectacular. I thought I saw Maggie float past but I can't be sure with the moonlight bouncing off the waves. It could just have easily been a white carrier bag. They seem to be plaguing the earth these days.

Eyes on You

"5,4,3,2,1 eyes on me."

You stood in the centre of the school hall, as sixty year 1s froze, in a trance, their heads turned towards you. My eyes were on you too but I wasn't waiting for instruction. I knew what to do. Every night, alone in my bed, you were in my arms. Tonight, I knew I would have to make a move. I'd been patient.

I saw you yesterday at school. You smiled and I knew something was different. You did that thing where you pretend you're looking at the children but really, you are seeking me out. I was there for quite a while watching you but I held back, behind the other parents, until most of them had retrieved their children and were making their way out of the school gates.

With practised timing, I stepped forward. You beamed at me, swept your long fringe away from your eyes with your right hand and tucked it neatly behind your ear. So you could see me better. I came over to you and took my daughter's hand but she wanted to play with a child who was still in the yard, so off she went and I was left less than a foot away from you. I could smell your perfume. Expensive; I wear the same one. *Now.*

"How are you?" you asked me with your concerned face. You'd remembered I'd been ill.
"I'm ok now, thanks," you looked deep into my eyes but it was my turn to pretend I was looking at the children and I glanced away. I wanted to ask if you fancied a coffee, away from where people knew us. We wouldn't want anyone getting the *right* idea now would we? I looked back at you but you had already moved towards the school entrance, where you would shut the door behind you and on us, for another evening. I felt my heart sink but knew I could get your attention when I dropped my daughter off the next morning. Not too long to wait, I consoled myself. I could also prepare what I was going to say.

"See you tomorrow, Caroline." I called over. I shouldn't have used your first name in front of the children but how could I resist hinting to the world that we knew each other intimately? You were busy with a demanding parent, who had obstructed your passage back into school. I could see you didn't want to be speaking with her and would have rather stayed with me. I shouldn't have pretended I was disinterested. What had I been thinking? I bet that upset you. I shouted over to my daughter, in one last attempt to get your attention. Laurel came running over and we started walking towards the school gates, at a slow pace.

"Mrs … um … Mrs McAllister!" I remember thinking; I bet you can sing with your lovely voice. You ran over, desperate to catch me. You were going to ask me for that drink, I was sure of it. The weeks had been building up to this.

"Hi sorry Mrs …"

"Call me Sarah, no need to be so formal out of school." I winked.

That threw you. You blushed and stammered out the next thing you said.

Mrs … er … Sar… when you said you would see me tomorrow, did you mean when you drop Laurel off, or were you planning on coming in to help? *Again.* It's just, if it's the latter … well, we, um … we don't need any more parent helpers in year 1!" She blurted out the last part.

"Oh, I see," I said. Well I didn't at all *see,* because Kai's mother goes into the school as a 'parent helper' and she started in November and I began helping in the October *before* her. She is still going into your classroom, each week. In fact, she told me last week that you had *specifically* asked her if she could!

I felt winded. I had to take a deep breath, so my facial expression wasn't betrayed by my inner thoughts! In that brief moment it took to contain myself, I understood what was going on. You clearly wanted to divert attention away from *us*. I didn't say this out loud, especially with Laurel there. Instead, I said with my most confident of smiles, that I understood and I would see if year 2 wanted a helper.

I was testing you of course; to gauge your reaction but you didn't say anything. I could tell you were trying to hide your feelings for me. Well, you needed to try harder, because it was obvious how you felt.

5,4,3,2,1 and breath! I popped into the school office first thing the next day and they were glad to have me in year 2! As luck would have it, there was a year 1 and 2 joint event being held in the school hall, which *you* were leading. I could see your face when I walked in with the year 2s. You went pink for sure and looked down for a second, as if gathering yourself. I felt it too.

You avoided me, the best you could, all afternoon and you weren't there when I collected Laurel, which was very unusual. I know your timetable. No reason why you shouldn't have been there. It made me smile, as you were clearly struggling with your feelings for me. I thought *I* was transparent but you …

I realised there and then, that I would have to make the first move, as I could see you weren't capable. I planned to drive over to your house later and talk everything through.

5,4,3,2,1 and take a deep breath. I have blood on my shoes. I can see it, even in this light. The orange street lighting makes it look like a blob of black tar on the light suede. I'm never going to get the stain out. They were my best ones as well. Designer. I wanted to look gorgeous for you and you always commented on my shoes. Never mind, without you to impress I guess I can dump them too. Far away from here though; at least I have learned something from Patricia Cornwall.

I really thought you wouldn't knock me back and that when confronted, you would acknowledge your true feelings for me and actually stop lying to me *and* yourself. They are just shoes but it is really annoying, my bloody footprints everywhere. As if I don't have enough to think about!

I only took the knife as backup but you left me no choice. Why did you have to say you would go to the police? I'm not a stalker! You made it very clear you liked me. For months I knew. No, you *weren't* just being friendly. What bollocks! I knew you were having a wobble because everyone thought you were straight. You didn't want to leave your husband for a woman, even though you loved me. I get it. This is basically what it comes down to, you, having second thoughts. Well too late sweetheart. I had plans.

You said I'd been driving past your house every night and your husband had been questioning you. Well, he should have been concerned; you were having an affair with me! We may not have physically acted on our feelings but the thought was there, which is just as bad. It's still adultery. You were just scared of the unknown. I know you love me.

You were easy to find. You knew you would be. That's why you gave me clues; you enjoyed the chase. You told me you lived at the coast. All I had to do was go on line and look on the electoral roll. I had to pay but it was worth it. I found your address straight away. Not the kind of house I expected, I have to say. It must have been *his* choice. I know what you like, don't I? You would have been happier with me.

I waited until I knew you were alone and knocked on your door. You seemed surprised. I couldn't believe you wouldn't let me in. I don't think anyone heard my raised voice and the names I called you before it happened. I only reacted to what you said to me. What did you expect? I'm not going to be strung along for you to then make out it was all my doing! Lying bitch!

Why did you say those things, making out it was all in my head and threatening to tell people? How could you betray me? My heart's in pieces! We could have had a lovely life together, just you and me. We didn't need anyone else. Laurel would have gone to live with her dad.

All you had to do was leave a goodbye note, with your key and get in the car with me. Everything would have fallen into place but you had to have a complete meltdown and say those things to me. I'm no psycho!

Anyway, it is what it is. You're lying at my feet languishing. I only pushed the knife in once. It penetrated your chest much easier than I'd imagined it would. When you fell back, I didn't loosen my grip of the handle and the blade slipped out of you, even easier than when it went in. The blood trickled at first, then gushed out and I couldn't stop it. To be honest I didn't try to. Are you sorry for your lies now?

Your skin is almost translucent, as your blood soaks your clothes and pools around your body like an oil slick. You ask me to help you and I crouch down so my face touches yours. I kiss your lips. I tell you I have to finish it; I'm not going to be blamed for your actions.

5,4,3,2,1 - pupils fixed and dilated.

The street lamp gifts you an orange halo. *My angel.* I will miss you at school.

Moon Dance

Something isn't right. Something I can't quite put my finger on. Something that sends a chill down my back, like a snake slithering along my spine, with its cool, dry skin.

I reach out to touch her but her side of the bed is empty and cold. Barren wasteland.

It's early hours of the morning and I wander, aimlessly, around the house. I stop to pour myself a drink. My throat, dry and scratchy, welcomes the tepid water as a dusty road welcomes rain. There's a deep ache forming at the back of my head.

The shadows outside begin to play tricks with my mind. Dark shapes rise and fall, dart in and out, spreading across the blue ground as the full moon smiles down on the lawn. A light breeze sways the trees, ruffles the longer blades of grass and swirls a few stray summer leaves. I can hear nature waking, birds singing their early morning call.

My heart thumps as icy tendrils squeeze my chest. Goose bumps spread down my arms and I drop the glass. It shatters into a million white sparkling jewels, glinting across the black ceramic floor, shimmering, where water pools.

I see her. Her shadow disappears behind a collection of pines, which flank the bottom of the garden.

She appears again dancing, a simple black shadow. I'm unable to make out her features but I know it's her. Her movement, her mannerisms, they're committed to my memory. Even at a distance, she compares exactly.

I could watch forever and never realise the time. Full of life she dances around the trees. I'm mesmerised. A pain rests heavy in my stomach, like I've swallowed a stone.

Moonlight strokes her soft, long blonde hair as it glides effortlessly. It highlights her shoulders, her dress, her shape, before the darkness swiftly takes her again. I search until my eyes ache. She's gone and all my hope is gone with her. I remain at the window, waiting, watching, wondering. Will I ever get another glimpse of her?

Nights like this are rare, precious, and I cherish every moment. To see her beauty and grace fills me with joy. The way she throws back her head as she laughs. The ways she reaches up to gently stroke back her hair. The way she crosses her feet as she twirls.

I may be romanticising, as I reflect on the good, through these rose tinted glasses I'm so fond of wearing. That's all I have left.

The gloom isn't in the room I'm standing in or in the dark corners where cobwebs lie or in the mist hovering inches above the lawn. The gloom lives in the deepest crevices of my mind. It isn't the tricks the moonlight plays, it's the tricks my mind plays, which are the worst.

My will alone can't conjure her up surely. Is she real? Or is she just a fragment of my own distressed imagination?

I'm lost in thought of many moons ago. Happier times when my world was full of life and love. When her smile lit up her face, as it lit up my heart. Happier times, before the tide and the dark, deep sea took her last breath away. And took her from me. The sea took a big part of me that day too, it left a hollow shell.

She loved swimming, almost as much as she loved dancing, especially at night. She loved how the moonlight skimmed the sea, lighting the way.

There's something about moonlight. It released the spirt within her. It took me by surprise, every time. Her eyes shone as her smile reflected through them, then I knew she was really alive. She knew it too. She became herself.

I don't realise I'm crying until I feel my cheeks are damp. It does nothing to sooth my aching heart.

I feel the glow and warmth of a thousand suns flood the room. As I turn towards the door, she's there, with her dress blowing gently in the breeze. Her feet are bare. She steps forward, one carefully placed foot at a time. She make no sound. She walks up to me gently and takes away my pain.

Later, much later, I feel the warmth of her body on mine as she slowly slips her arms around my neck, holding me close, for a second time. She kisses me with urgency, and holds me tight as if she's afraid to let me go. I'm certain, I never want to let her go. I know now, she's real.

My storm passes, for now. Until the morning and she disappears in to the depths where ghostly shadows go in daylight hours.

My aim has always been to live in the moment; to embrace the here and now. Forget the past. Don't dwell on dreams that may or may not materialise in the future, dreams are all they can be.

Now I find myself waiting, hoping and living my life in limbo. It has been a decade and I can't bring myself to break the last connection, no matter how tenuous the link.

I wait a whole year before the moonlight casts its spell on the garden. She's come, at last. She appears from the behind the pines, dances, moves deftly to her own tune. I feel inanimate. I have waited so long, I fear she will leave me broken hearted once again.

Sudden warmth, floods through the room. Relief fills me. She's glowing in the moonlight. She steps forward, leaving ghostly prints behind, which evaporate, on the cool black tiles.

Tonight, today, our wedding anniversary, she utters no words of love. Not a single vow or promise pass her lips. It's simple. I feel her love as she walks up to me so gracefully, kisses me so fully and takes my crown of thorns.

Inspired by Bob Dylan's 'Shelter from the Storm'.

In the Shadow of the Dome

The wind snarled at us when we arrived and the rain was so torrential, we camped in the B&B for three days, venturing out only for meals. Today, the landlady mentioned the children being off school, so I said that they had different holidays down south. She seemed satisfied with that, not that it's any of her business. Anyway, it could be true. Where we lived before, children were always being taken out of school. The ski-set were the worst. Every March, the week or so before the end of term, children would be whipped out of lessons in their droves, to fly off to the Alps. Well, I have never taken my children out of school for anything other than illness. They were better off there.

Samuel says he wants to go back but Lucy hasn't mentioned anything. She's more aware. I feel utterly wretched about that but she is away from it now. We all are.

I sense a shift in mood today. The sun is helping. The sky isn't quite Mediterranean blue; there are a few wispy clouds but they harbour no threat of rain. No, today is the day we begin our lives again. I wiggle my toes in the surf. Dog walkers occasionally jog past us with smiles and hellos but no one else is here.

The Dome, a local landmark, stands in the distance, with spectacular opulence on the golden sand, like a white diamond nestled in its crown. A light breeze touches my hair. The children hop in and out of rock pools, just feet away, giggling. God, when did I last hear them laugh? White foam sways in and out, mimicking the rhythm of my heart beat. No more fight or flight; I feel almost relaxed.

Lucy tenses as her attention turns to something behind me. I swing round to look. Two police cars have parked on the top road – lights flashing. Several police officers are heading down the stone steps onto the beach. Lucy yanks Samuel's hand, pulling him towards me. She knows what this means but Samuel is upset he has left his bucket by the rocks.

The breeze is chilly on my arms and the clouds are gathering. I think it might rain. I want to fight and I want to run but instead I hug my children, as tight as they can bear. In my head I am screaming at the advancing uniforms, *he is the one to blame with his punches and threats; he's the one who bullies and scares the children!* But I say nothing. A solicitor will have to do my talking and make them see it was entirely *his* fault. I stand, stoic, on the sand with my babies, an inglorious landmark; a memorial for injustice, because they are coming to arrest *me*, not *him* - my husband.

My husband is currently 300 miles away, lying on our kitchen floor with a bread knife through his throat but I am guilty of nothing.

Living words

Chills spread, as I turn the first page,
Dreich and dreary splutter and spill,
Eerie, ferocious and grey,
Literally, jumps from the spine at will.

The mist rolls in, twisting and tumbles,
Right off the end of my hunched up knees.
Iridescent, inky splodged, clouds linger
And fills my head with drizzle and unease.

Yellow haze spews where wet cobbles shine
Transported to a deserted back-lane.
Nestled, revealing within the pages of crime
Delving, diving, deeper the delivery of pain.

Banging, breaking and smashing
The whip cracking wonder of thunder.
Lightning strikes, bursting out of confines.
The knife does its dirty deed, without blunder.

Killer on the loose, running, running,
Slinking seamlessly into the night.
Cops don't know which way to turn.
Mr & Mrs expire, dead, lying in plight.

Blood smears, squelches and splatters,
Soaks deep, carpet fibres like dye.
Blood glints, shining, silky smooth,
Misty moonlight beams from the sky.

The next page flutters revealing,
Clean rooms. Blood is all gone.
Forensics comb, crawl and sweep.
Appearing simple, in one easy turn.

A girl and a dog in morning's soft glow,
Walk blindly into the park.
With the cold skies warning to all,
Radiant sparkling days, are marked.

Innocently unaware of the danger
Her world is about to fatally unfold.
Dreich and dreary penetrates again.
Rustling pages reveal the story to be told.

Will he be caught or will he go on?
A knife, he uses with ease and abandon.
Seeking, searching, is it futile?
Serial murderer takes lives in random

I'm there, I pretend.
Thrilling excitement I spend.
I don't want, 'The end'.

Forsaken

My face is plastered all over the national papers today, it's moved on from me just being a local celebrity. Sandy, two doors along, was chirping on about it. I really don't get what the big deal is. Anyway, all the details are wrong. Just like the press to sensationalise something really quite mundane and un-newsworthy. They punked up the whole story. I think Sandy wishes it was him. Likes the idea of being famous; he's such a pain in the arse. All of them round here hang onto his every word, like he actually knows what he's talking about. Bet he wishes he had done it though but he'd never say – too weak. They all are.

It takes guts to stand up and tell it how it is. I understand what Jesus went through now, cast out, and made a fool of, just to get his beliefs out there. You've either got it, or you haven't, I say. These idiots can point and jeer all they like but they feel exactly the same as me on the inside. If they want to crucify me for being honest about it, fine. Dickheads, all of them!

It's the parents that get me every time. Their attitude is hilarious, like they don't have a clue what their kids are up to. Their *innocent* children totally stitched me up, that's what! They probably thought it would get them off the hook and didn't think how going to the police and telling stories, with their embellishments can ruin someone's life. Proper drama queens they are. Totally unnecessary!

Oh, there he goes again, Sandy calling me to his cronies. I can hear him outside my door. Gav, opposite mine, thinks Sandy's a nonce and pointing at me the way he does, takes the eyes off him. Maybe. I don't think he could pull anything other than what's in his pants! At least I'm always sure it's what these young women want! I'm no paedo. Those pervs are scum. My situation is totally different and they know it. I think the papers must have offered a lot of money for their false allegations.

I blame that singer, whatshername? And those like her. It's people like her that encourages girls to look and dress like they do. Nail varnish, short skirts, those crop top things and loads of red lipstick. What do they think's going to happen eh? Would you wave a slab of raw meet in front of a hungry dog and expect it not to lick it, at least? Fucking hypocrites!

It was ok until my niece's step daughter decided she would make more of a thing of it. Told her dad all sorts, after I babysat. I can only imagine. She's far from a baby, that one. Called me upstairs saying she'd had a nightmare; wanted me to lie next to her and comfort her. I really don't think that eight years old is too young to be culpable. I could marry her in EastanBoo, or wherever it is. I think we all just need to calm down and look at the facts. She *wanted* me to do it and said nothing at the time that made me think different.

What would they say about the six year old that came onto me in the park? At least they haven't a clue about that one. She knew it was her doing you see, kept her mouth shut.

My solicitor said I should be all right in here, if I to go into solitary for a bit. No way! I've done nothing wrong, I told him. Put those silly little tarts on the stand I said, only then people can judge what really happened. Apparently they were too young for that as well. So their statements and some dodgy evidence got me banged up. The world's gone mad.

I can hear the guards coming round to lock up. Sounds like a few of them are heading my way. I don't think it's my autograph they're wanting. I have been expecting this if I'm honest. Forsaken, just like Christ.

Devine Intervention

My plans to escape are futile.

Today, my wedding day, should be the happiest day of a young girl's life. I imagine for most young girls, it is. Even if the gentleman prize of husband is not sufficient to guarantee happiness; the planning of a party to celebrate, usually affords a degree of excitement and expectant fun.

Alas, life does take such an unfortunate turn of events, which provide far reaching effects and best laid plans, often fall by the wayside.

As for my wedding day being the happiest day of my life, I suppose, in a perverse way it is.

While typhoid is not the way anyone would choose to go, it does, for me, provide an unexpected escape route. It has saved me from executing my own elaborate plans for my permanent release from my obligations; for my demise.

Paramount, is ensuring I do not break the agreement my family entered into. Luckily for us, unlucky for him, he insisted that *'his dear Hannah'* move into his home a good few months ahead of the wedding. To broker the deal, and to get his own way, the bride price was paid in full. My family's future secured. It is the deviousness of such a deal which enables me to put my own plans in to place.

With trepidation I arrived at Calverstone Castle in the March of 1893 with my meagre suitcase in hand. My first impression was of grandeur, which was as obscene as the gargoyles surrounding the perimeter of the grounds; the intent to scare young vagrants from the premises was evident. I almost requested my driver turn around, with the smell of my own perspiration and fear bemoaning an acute premonition, but I am rather quite timid and we rode onward.

I consider myself plain, not quite ugly, but I have no features anyone would call pretty. I know other girls admire my long, wavy, chestnut locks, which I have long since found quite tiresome. But with no other redeeming features to speak of, I retain my locks in a bid to detract from the simplicity of my face.

Despite my demeanour, Mr Forshaw seemed quite taken with *'his dear Hannah'.* His appreciation was chivalrous, at first, but it became most apparent that his graciousness was to be short lived. No sooner had I unpacked my small array of dresses was his meanness evident.

To my astonishment, and for no reason that I could understand; I awoke to raise my head from the pillow and found my hair did not come with me. The Master had taken scissors to my locks as I slept soundly in my Chamber.

Clarity pronounced soon after; his expectation of my intimate wifely duties outlined and, with surprise, demonstrated, before my dress was even stitched! His breath, foul and putrid with the sting of brandy and cigars, bore down on my face. My dress and undergarments ripped and un-repairable, taking what he stated was '*his right',* as I '*belong'* to him. Obliterating the romance of the earlier period forever. The pain I endured, as he held me down, against my protests, his voice ferocious, as he snarled; "No one else will have you now, used, dirty, unattractive; with no beautiful hair left you look unappealing, you disgust me.” He seemed quite expert in inflicting emotional and physical pain, and had a surprising unending, arsenal of wickedness at his disposal.

He is a brutal and ignorant old man. A man who has already shown me three of his many faces. A man whose reputation is well established amongst the gentile women folk of our society. Marriage would be, simply, intolerable. To my shame it is well known that he has taken women for his own selfish amusement, against their will. He bears no remorse or reprisal. Marriage under these arrangements would be, I am convinced, a fate worse than my own unforeseen circumstances.

I am aware that my surroundings are rather plush and for that I am thankful for this small mercy. Money has been scarce for Mother and Father, which is why I am in this plight. Father’s business became difficult in recent years. Our lovely family home rcquires extensive repairs to ensure it remains habitable for my younger brother and sisters. Financial assistance was desperately required. I am the only one who could help. So, I agreed to sacrifice myself, with the love and friendship of my dearest family being at the forefront of my mind.

An unquestionably simple, young mind I am regularly reminded. Yet, if others deem my mind to be so simple, how would I know such a thing? I have no other mind with which to compare it. Daydreaming, I am told, is my favoured pastime. Although I do not consider myself to be such a daydreamer. I rather prefer to think I exercise my poor simple mind in order to, well, help it be not so simple. Devising plots and plays to amuse, primarily myself, and on occasion others, is more fulfilling than being tethered to the embroidery frame, or enduring endless dreary chatter of boys, with pretty little innocents.

Death does not become a lady, or so Mother states, unknowingly. While the degradation and humility of the act itself, being wholly reliant on the maid and nursing staff, did provide at times, a reddened face, the means does definitely justify the end.

So, I feel today is the day that death does, most certainly, most handsomely and most beautifully, become a lady. Death serves me very well and most richly. Escaping his presence, in a way even the new Mr Houdini would find difficult to master. For me, it is a necessity.

I rush my escape with such enthusiasm and as much grace as I did in my early days of childhood. Hovering, rather unsteadily and ungainly, I look down at my desiccated and redundant body. I feel a release from the confines of an ill and tortured shell. My intolerable pain that rendered me useless and immobile, has evaporated.

The nurse lays a penny on each eyelid and carefully pulls the white linen bedsheet over my body. She walks calmly, I observe, to the window and opens it, as I'm sure she would be trained, to release my spirit upon my death. Release to where, I'm unsure, as I have no place to go, not yet anyway. Before she leaves my bed chambers, she stops, turns to look at me and with a small curtsey, crosses herself, before rushing for the door.

My Master, Mr Forshaw, is not present, I notice. Presumably attending to more important matters than being by my side in my hour of need. I lay entombed for 3 whole week, in my once pretty chamber, as the reek of death and decay exudes all around me. Bit by bit, my body, twisted in pain, as the poisonous bacteria ran through me. Mr Forshaw has not touched me, or ventured in my vicinity, since the fever began. Yet, I heard him in the grounds below my window taking his morning walks, giggling playfully, with whichever mistress he favoured that day.

Lily, my personal maid, is standing still in the corner of the room. She's so quiet I almost over look her. I find her gently sobbing, small tears run down her cheeks. I have known her such a short time but we became friendly from my first day at Calverstone Castle. She is such a gentle caring soul. I sigh, as Lily's tears touch my heart.

Surprisingly, a rush of uncontrollable exhilaration, sends me flying across to the other side of my chamber. With all the grace of an infant, I crash into my dressing table, knocking my favourite things which tumble to the floor with a loud bump.

Lily looks up, with wide eyes and surveys the broken looking glass. The sweet smell of perfume masks the rancid odour of my diseased corps as it wafts through the air. My bottles and soft bristle hair brush, scatter about her feet. Her tears stop suddenly. Her usual rosy cheeks turn as pale as the linen covering my lifeless body. As she cries out, involuntarily, she startles herself into motion.

Lily's scream alarms me, as I lie stunned and awkward on the dressing table. I am unsure of how it happened. Lily's reaction is perplexing. Could she see me I wonder? Is that what frightened her? Or did she simply come to the only conclusion possible, that it is me, who caused such destruction? I wish poor Lily no ill will but, oh, this is going to be such fun! I wonder how loyal she'll be now.

Before Lilly escapes from the room I ask, "Help me Lily, will you help me?" Lily stops, looking about her in bewilderment, with eyes as big as a frightened fox. She can hear me. I think I hear her whisper, as she answers positively, before she hurries from the room.

The reality is magnificent. A partner in crime perchance? My plans know no bounds. Free at last to do as I please, to roam hither and tither; playing

childish games whenever and wherever I wish. Even with such a simple mind as mine to please.
For now, I rest. While I have never been mean-spirited, on this occasion, I think I will find the wear-with-all to administer meanness most easily.

My dearest, detested fiancé, please don't ever expect to find contentment. I am about to unleash my own fun to liven up your life, in ways you can't even begin to imagine. Hold on to your sanity, my betrothed. You are going to need all of the strength you can muster. I will show you no mercy.

Tomorrow begins the haunting of your life and I am going to scare you to your untimely and humiliating death.

At the end of the day

He shouted down to me that his calves were killing him. I'd forgotten about his knee operation. I brought him down the easiest way, in my opinion, but I suppose we could have gone down the stairs and he would have had the handrail. The bank down to the Fish Quay is particularly steep.

I looked round and he'd sat down at a picnic table outside of the Low Lights Tavern. I walked back up to his grumpy face.

It was such a beautiful, warm day, as we sat in the open air bronzing our cheeks. I went bright red of course but he was browning like a baked potato. I thought he would complain about the heat but he was too involved with his pie - dissecting it. He ate next to nothing, so I finished his off. He had the steak and ale with mushy peas and mash and I had the chicken and mushroom with chips and beans. Delicious washed down with a small ale. He had water, said he was too thirsty for alcohol. I had hoped he would've had a drink to limber him up a bit. I know my legs feel looser after a beer. We sat for a while, after the plates had been taken away. I asked him if he could recall the pies we had the first time we went there years ago. He could.

We took our time getting down to the river and braved the seagulls stalking the ice cream van and those folks with their takeaways. Even though I was full from lunch, my mouth watered from that familiar smell of fried loveliness, gorged in salt and vinegar.

"Should we have a walk into Tynemouth?" I asked. I got a look which implied I'd forgotten about his knees again. I hadn't but I thought he should get some exercise. It was mainly flat, I reassured him. Until of course one reached the steep bank or two at the other end but I *forgot* to remind him of those. I bribed him with a latte and cake at Woods and we were off. He was like a mountain goat up the hills at the end. Liked his desserts.

All out of puff he was. Said he was desperate for a sit down and he plonked himself on the sofa. He said he wanted to sit indoors out of the sun. I was pleased as my forehead was burning. I went to order. I fancied carrot cake but that had all gone, so I settled for coffee and walnut. He wanted a rocky road but said his eyes had been bigger than his tummy, when it arrived. Both of us had the hot chocolate with all the trimmings. I asked for more squirty cream, saying it had evaporated before I had a chance to enjoy it. So untrue of course but it made him chuckle like it always did and he teased me about my sweet tooth. He was usually just as bad. Not today though. He said it was the heat.

We had a stroll along Front Street, then down to King Edwards Bay. I fancied Longsands Beach then tea at the Grand but he said if we were planning to walk back to Shields, he wouldn't have the strength in his knees to do both.

We had a lovely walk on the sand and he took his socks off so we could plodge. I saw the boy in his eyes as he laughed. The boy I married.

"Nothing like the sea breeze to blow away the cobwebs," I said. He put his arm round me and we sat for a while looking out to see. We didn't speak. We didn't need to.

He asked if we could skip the Grand and maybe go home. He said he wanted me all to himself. I joked and said he'd had me to himself for 34 years.

The sun was going down as we walked back past Collingwood's monument to the Fish Quay. That was when he told me. He said it so matter of fact. I said I thought it was his knees. "Terminal," he said.

I've not been back since. Such a nice warm day and I thought it would do me good. I'm sitting outside the Staith House though. I came down the stairs to avoid the Low Lights Tavern … I don't fancy pie.

There will be cake

Her mouth worked furiously, she was a frog gasping for air, as she lay on the floor dying. My Gran, Evie, had looked better. I realised it was serious when her lips turned blue. That's when I knew it wasn't good.

Uncle Jay and Cousin Gordon were trying to help by loosening the top button on her pink, floral blouse. One of them grabbed a tea towel and started fanning her like she was hot out of the oven. Her hair took on a life of its own; it was caked in hairspray, so it moved all in one go.

Gran wasn't a fan of wearing her teeth, not the bottom set anyway, but today she had neither. She had taken them out earlier after a bit of meat from a ham and pea's pudding sandwich got stuck and she couldn't get it out. She stuffed her teeth in her bra, as usual, so she didn't lose them and, as a result, her grin was all gummy.

I could tell the dynamic duo were reluctant to give her the kiss of life. They wrestled with each other; heads bobbing and egging each other on. Neither Uncle Jay nor Cousin Gordon made any movement to pucker up. They were flapping so much I thought they were going to take off at one point.

My boyfriend, Rory, a thick set lad; thick in every sense of the word as it happens, was standing over her. Not that he would know what to do to help. Slightly inebriated; he was swaying and bending over her, with a bottle of San Miguel in his hand. He was breathing fumes in her face like a dragon in a brewery.

Rory looked directly at me. He raised his thumb on his right hand. My breath caught in my chest; pure relief, she's going to be ok. He raised his thumb up higher then swiftly plunged it sharply down, like a Tern diving after a fish. With an upside down smile on his face he shook his head. What the fuck? What a dickhead he can be! If I could've got my friggin' hands on him at that very moment, dead Granny or not, I would have kicked the fucking shit out of him. He'd have been black and blue for weeks. Stupid moron. Having the news delivered like that was hardly going to make the party go with a swing.

Minutes before she fell to the floor Evie was sitting on a chair; skirt hitched up, legs akimbo, with her stockings and bloomers on full display. Not that anyone paid any attention. We'd seen it all before. Singing at the top of her voice, sherry in hand, for 'medicinal purposes, you know,' she winked. 'Knees up Mother Brown' was her favourite. Nothing to do with her maiden name being Evie Brown. She got excited when she sang along, splashing a bit of her sherry down herself while swaying and stamping her foot. Spilling her sherry was unheard of, a mortal sin, but she didn't seem to notice. She was too busy smiling, toothlessly, it made her look like she was either as happy as a sand dancer with bats in the attic, or grimacing like a strange ventriloquist's doll - it was hard to tell.

There seemed to be a bit of confusion between Uncle Bob and Uncle Jay. While Evie lay in between them, prostrate on the floor, an argument started. Hands were waving above her and Guinness slopped on to Evie while she lay helpless. I'm glad they understood each other as no one else could at the best of times.

Uncle Jay stood on one side of Gran and Uncle Bob on the other, both red in the face. They never really did see eye to eye and Evie spent her life pulling them apart. That's twins for you.

Uncle Bob began to roll up his sleeves, so I was expecting some argybargy. Cousin Gordon, usually a hot-headed dick at the best of times, stepped in, so I was ready for the punches to fly. Cousin Gordon grabbed them both by the scruff of the neck, in a slow calculated movement, pulled them in close. At the last minute, and as quick as a flying fart, he banged their heads together. Hard. I could hear the crack echo around the room, above the music.

"What the fuck …?"

"Arsehole."

"Twat."

"Wanker."

"Knob jockey."

Cousin Gordon took it without flinching and didn't loosen his grip. He moved his head, near to theirs when they stopped shouting and muttered something to them both. Uncle Bob turned away and Uncle Jay dropped his head down. What the hell did he say? No one could knew except the three of them.

Both Uncles looked each other in the eyes, smiled and nodded. To everyone's surprise they'd reached an early resolution, if there ever was a disagreement, it was quickly forgotten like a turd flushed down the loo. Cousin Gordon puffed up; all pleased with himself, because it was exactly what Evie would have done to sort them out.

Keen to keep the party going, Uncle Bob ushered us all into the next room, with his bony fingers grasped tight on his pint, he still hadn't let go of his Guinness.
"Ah, come on, Unc?" Molly said, "We can't go on as if nothing's happened. It's your Ma for God sake."
"Course we can, Moll! Don't be such a big, daft lass. Ya Granny loved a party. The last thing she would want to do is to spoil it for us."

Everyone moved to the next room. Cousin Gordon carried a crate of Stella under his arm and shouted at me to get the 'tunes'. I stuck my middle finger up at him and told him to 'go swivel'; shrugging I turned away. Who does he think he is? Just because he's a year older than me, it gave him no right to boss me about.

The ambulance and the paramedics arrived five minutes later, too late, since it had been well publicised that she was a goner. They checked her over all the same, but only confirmed what Rory had indicated.

The paramedics didn't take her away, I didn't realise that wasn't part of their routine. We had to wait for the undertakers to come. With no idea how long it would take for the black, private ambulance to turn up, it was decided we couldn't leave her lying on the floor – someone might trip over her or anything. It was Cousin Gordon's idea – two idea's in one day from him was astounding. So it was decided, and we popped her back on the chair.

Apart from the mild interruption, the party was in full swing. Uncle Bob spilled his Guinness all over the place, doing a strange 'Dad dance' where he bent his knees, stuck his bum out and flapped his elbows. I'm sure he thinks every dance is the birdy dance. It's the only one he knows the moves to, but he was out of time and sang out of tune.

A knock at the door signalled the arrival of the undertakers. Cousin Gordon to the rescue again shouted for the music to be turned down;
"Quit the tunes lads, have a bit of fucking respect for the old girl!" And surprisingly they all did as he said.
I opened the door on the two sombre men with a trolley and led them in to the back room where Evie was waiting.

There is always one, isn't there? Every party has them, some strange bloke that no one knows. He was sitting in the back room talking to Gran. I caught him offering her a swig from his bottle of lager. I looked at the undertakers; they hesitated at the door as they took stock of the scene in front of them. Clearly, they tried to control their facial expressions.

Swiftly, poor old Gran was carried out by the two burly, handsome, young men in suits. Evie would have loved it; she loved a man dressed properly, tie and all. It's a pity she wasn't here to see it. Fortunately, someone had the presence of mind to pull the hem of her skirt down to cover her tea coloured stockings and her less than white bloomers. Not that she would have been bothered. Everyone had seen her bloomers from the milk man to the lad next door, and I'm not talking on the washing line. Not that she was a slapper or anything. God forbid!

Uncle Jay announced the food was open. "Since we've had a natural break, help yourselves to sausage rolls, volley thingies and cheese on little sticks. I think there's a pork pie or two for the veggies amongst us."

You couldn't hold them back, no queue or orderly fashion, just a good old free for all. Plates were passed over heads, pickled onions dropped on the floor and trodden in the carpet, crisps being snaffled and stuffed in their gobs before they've put anything on the plates. I even saw our Molly's boyfriend put peanuts in his pocket. He must've been saving them for later. They're all pigs when they eat. It's carnage. I've seen livestock with better table manners.

Once they'd all stuffed their faces, got another bottle of beer or a warm glass of white wine the music was turned up to full belt and the karaoke machine was plugged in. Before it got started, and requests were made, Uncle Bob asked if anyone wanted cake.

"My Ma makes the best Victoria sponge around here for miles."

Funnily enough, the cake lay untouched.

And I decided, if you can't beat them join them. Retrieving a bottle of red wine I'd hidden in the bush in the garden, I sat and got slowly pissed before singing 'Like a Virgin' on the karaoke, at the very top of my singing voice. Not quite 'Knees up Mother Brown' but Evie would have been a little bit proud of me, maybe! She'd even be slightly proud of Cousin Gordon, I think.

I imagine Evie watching from her perch with her foot tapping to the music.

I still think Cousin Gordon's a Fuckwit. But only I can call the numb nuts that, because he's one of us.

I haven't made my mind up about that thick, fucking nob-head, Rory. He's got a canny cock and he's not a bad lay. I'll probably keep shagging him until something better comes along. Besides we need him to help carry Evie's coffin. And at least he's handy to go to the bar.

The next do is the funeral. I wonder who will make the cakes now. Not me, that's for friggin' sure!

The Shrieking Woman

I heard my name being called from somewhere far away. A woman's voice; no one recognisable, youngish. Younger than me anyway. Then the stinging slap across my chest. I sat bolt upright in my bed and I remember the feeling of adrenalin in my blood and the breathlessness of fear taking hold of me, sweat tickling the back of my neck and spine. I looked around in the dim lit room of early morning. There was no one but me. A bad dream, nothing more. Then his scream. His ear-piercing six year old scream.

I was outside Ernie's room in seconds and as I threw open the door not knowing what to expect. My son was climbing down his ladder to run to me. A shaking little scrap of innocence; wet faced and terrified. I went to lift him down and he leaped onto me, sobbing.
"What's wrong Ernie?"
"The man, Mummy. In my bedroom! He tapped my shoulder and woke me up."
"Mummy will make it better. Come in my bed. It was just a dream, my beautiful boy."

And all was well, until the next time.

For Ernie and me, our usual life took over for three days and then darkness descended. We had an early dinner and a bath. Ernie was very tired. So we agreed he would have an early night. He had been sleeping in my bed since the bad dream. He was a restless sleeper and neither of us had got any descent sleep with us sharing a bed, so this particular night I popped him in his own bed hoping we would both get some rest. It took a bit of encouragement but he was soon asleep.

I decided to go to bed and read. I dozed off, drifting in and out of sleep. A woman called my name in my dream. It became louder. Then a shout. Then Ernie cried out. I found myself in his room.

"Mummy can I come in your bed? That man was in here again."

"It is just a dream darling. I will stay with you until you go back to sleep. Scooch over." I was still half asleep.

I lay in bed with my arms round him. I tried to move a couple of times but he stirred too much and protested.

"Stay with me Mummy."

I "shush-shushed" him and he went off again but each time I tried to move, the same thing would happen and I would lay back down to console him. Half an hour or so later, I began to feel very cold. I adjusted the single duvet over us both but it made no difference. I could see my breath in the air as I exhaled. Ernie was in a deep sleep at last, so I planned to go and check the thermostat as the heating obviously hadn't kicked in.

Before I could move, the hairs on the back of my neck prickled; someone was behind me. I felt a hard, cold, bony tap on my shoulder. I turned to look but no one was there. My heart raced. I picked Ernie up and we were in my bed with the door shut in a matter of seconds. I don't recall how I negotiated the ladder of his cabin bed, while carrying my child's heavy, sleeping body.

I put my bedside light on and lay there trying to rationalise what had happened. The room was warm and we cuddled up tightly. Despite trying not to, I fell into a deep sleep. Then it happened.

I woke up to a scream in my ear and a slap across my chest. It was unmistakable, the woman's shrill voice

echoed round the room, as I sat there fully awake. Ernie was gone. I dived out of bed and ran onto the landing calling his name. The unseen woman's screams persisted. I stood in the doorway of his bedroom. He was there. The room was freezing and I held out my hand calling his name as calmly as I could but he just stood, stark still. He had his back to me. I moved forward.
"Ernie, Mummy's here, come here love." I was shivering with the cold and fear.
His head turned slightly with the sound of my voice.

I called to him again. This time he turned all the way round. He had been crying. His eyes were dark and his gaze far away.
"The man wants me to go with him, Mummy."
There was a sudden overwhelming stench in the room. Ernie didn't react but it made me want to be sick. I covered my nose and mouth with my hand.
"Come here, Ernie, come to me." I tried to move forward but something stopped me. Cold invisible hands pushed me back. The woman's voice shrieked louder, close to my ear but it seemed to be echoing around the whole house. I shouted over the din for Ernie to walk to me.

“I can’t Mummy, he won’t let me.” From the shadows I saw him. It. Whatever it was, it stepped forward into the moonlit room, so I could see. It was a man ... but it wasn’t living. Its face was somewhere between life and death, hollow and pale. Its eyes were wide, dark, crazed. Grey matted patches of long, silver, hair sprouted from a scalp writhing with maggots and sores oozing with puss. He wore rags; dirty decaying clothes reminiscent of a suit.

I couldn’t discern from what era this being had manifested but it wasn’t of this earth, from this moment in time, of that I was certain. Its grinning wide mouth dribbled slime from a pustule coated tongue; black and serpentine, slithering and oscillating over broken, crooked teeth. It had no lips and slithers of grey skin hung from its cheekbones, as if ripped by something even more unimaginable. Raw-boned fingers, touched my son’s hair and I heard its malevolent chuckle, a man's voice but deeper, a growl from somewhere dark and soulless.
“Oh God, this isn’t happening, please help him, please help. Get the fuck away from him!” I was crying hysterically. He seemed to like that and laughed louder as my anguish intensified. The shrieking woman was

in the freezing room with us now and the chuckling stopped abruptly.
“Leave us, you interfering wench!” The creature’s voice spat out into the darkness.
A whisper at first, “He is not yours, he is not yours, he is not yours …” then she shrieked, “HE IS NOT YOURS!” A child’s voice frantically called for its mummy, but it was not *my* child. Ernie was silent and still.
“HE IS NOT YOURS!” she wailed at the being. “NO MORE, NO MORE, NO MORE …!”
“THE CHILD IS MINE, YOU INTERFERING WHORE!” He was shouting to the woman’s voice. “YOU COULDN’T STOP ME WHEN WE WALKED THIS EARTH TOGETHER AND YOU CAN’T STOP ME NOW. ALL CHILDREN IN THIS HOUSE ARE MINE, WHETHER THEY WERE EXPELLED FROM YOUR PUTRID CAVITY, OR NOT!”

The hold the demon had on my son was released. He ran to me screaming, arms in the air, wanting me to lift him. I swung him off the carpet and against me; my arms locked together around him. I heard the woman’s voice close to my ear.
“Run, run, run, run, run, run …”

I rushed to the stairs and the demon was swearing, shouting and threatening, behind us. I got to the front door and turned the key but it wouldn't open.
The woman screamed, "RUUUUUUUUUUUUN!" and the door handle released, effortlessly, in my hand.

I was in the street holding onto Ernie and I was crying, shouting for help, for someone to come. I looked back at the house and I saw her. I saw the woman. She was looking out of Ernie's bedroom window straight at me, on my knees, in the street below. She was young, pale. Translucent. She held a child of similar age to Ernie, a girl, I think. She smiled at me gently, which reached her kind but mournful eyes. Then she was gone.

A few neighbours came out of their houses and a Police car arrived. It all just seemed to happen at once. The neighbours said they had heard screaming and called the police. The police wanted to take me back inside but I begged them not to, so they interviewed me next door, at the Fitzpatrick's house.

Ernie said he had been asleep and when he woke I was screaming at him. He said it had happened a few times lately, that I tapped his shoulder and touched his hair, laughing and tormenting him, so he could not go to sleep. He said he was scared of me running through the house shrieking.

There was talk of stress since my husband moved out and raised eyebrows when I told them my version of events. There was a discussion about my having post-natal depression when Ernie was born and concerns that I never fully recovered. I remember social workers arriving with my husband and me being sedated, as they took Ernie. I remember begging to be believed. I remember it all happened that night.

They say that soon I will be able to go home. As long as I keep up my medication and counselling. I have made good progress, apparently. They say when I am settled, my son will one day be allowed to stay over and hopefully he will eventually come and live with me full time again.

My soon to be ex-husband put the house on the market and I will be renting for a while until the divorce settlement is sorted but I don't see why Ernie can't be with me straight away. We will be happy together. My ex says Ernie is scared of me but I know he will be ok once he knows the truth. I admitted to the doctors that it was the stress of losing my husband to a young blond; the sleepless nights brought on by worry and loneliness; the occasional drink …

I miss him. I have only seen Ernie twice a week since that night but he is safe. I don't mean safe from me, I would never harm him. He is safe from whatever demonic abomination wanted to take him away from me that night and I have only the shrieking woman to thank.

My being on this ward is small price to pay for his life but of course I won't tell the doctors that. No, I will be out soon. I just have to plan how to get Ernie back from that poor excuse of a father who has turned him against me.

Orchids

The curtains are closed as Sally arrives. The modest 1930's, red brick house is in darkness. She's unsure if she has the right time; but Mrs Wilson has her hair done this time every fortnight. Sally knocks, not expecting an answer. The door opens and Mrs Wilson is her usual bright self; "Come in lovely, I've been waiting for you."

Sally walks in to the hall. "I didn't know if you would be in. I thought I might have the wrong time. With your curtains drawn I thought you must be away."
"Oh that? Yes, yes, I mean … no. It's my husband; he's dead."
"Aw, no, I'm sorry. I can come back some other time. You just let me know when you want me to come back. Any time you prefer." Sally talks with rapid fire.
"No, dear, I need my hair done now. Look at the state of it!" Mrs Wilson ruffles her short grey waves to prove her point.

Sally walks down the hallway tentatively. Usually she pulls her hairdressing trolley behind her but she is leaning over it as she pushes it in front of her. She

sniffs the air and glances around into rooms, furtively, as she passes open doorways.
“What are you doing?” Mrs Wilson walks slowly behind her.
Sally jumps. “I’m … he’s … I’m … I’m wondering if, erm, I mean, is … he … still in the house?”
Mrs Wilson laughs loudly, “No, don’t be daft, we had the funeral yesterday.”

Sally, relieved, sets up her hairdressing kit in the kitchen. As she busies herself she notices through the half closed blinds a large display of flowers in the garden. Mrs Wilson catches her peering out at them; “Come on, come and have a look; they’re beautiful.”

Sally follows Mrs Wilson into the garden and a magnificent display of flowers are arranged over the dark soil of the flower beds. Except, they’re not planted in the garden, they’re lying on the soil; in bunches and wreaths.

Sally’s palms sweat and she’s not sure what to say or do. Feeling she has to say something, as Mrs Wilson is looking at her expectantly. “They’re beautiful.

Beautiful colours. But … I've … never heard of anyone bring the flowers home?"
"They would have gone to waste dear, so my son said I should keep them. After all, people have spent a lot of money on them. Aren't they gorgeous?"
"Yes, they are." Sally is reeling, dumbstruck, but thinks she needs to show enthusiasm, and adds, "Particularly the orchids." As her eye catches a large wreath in pink and white.

As swift as an eagle Mrs Wilson swoops down and picks up the wreath. "Here, you have it. You must. I've got so many." Sally tries to refuse, politely of course as she has no intention of insulting Mrs Wilson, especially since she's usually a good tipper.

Mrs Wilson leaves the wreath, by the sink after topping up the oasis with water to keep them fresh for Sally to take home.

Sally finishes Mrs Wilson's hair, packs up her trolley and makes to leave without the flowers. Mrs Wilson with her quick instincts reaches for the flowers and insists Sally takes them, pushing them in to her hand.

Sally has another few appointments that afternoon and as she's driving she feels uneasy about the floral tribute and keeps glancing over at it on the back seat of her car. She feels a shiver sweep through her. Shaking her head, she tells herself she's just being stupid. They're only flowers.

The next night Sally and her husband, William, have friends coming over for dinner. Sally, busy in the kitchen marinating and what not, nips in to the dining room and sets the table for six, with plenty of time to spare. She retreats to the kitchen to complete the preparations.

An hour later Sally returns to the dining table to set out condiments and notices that the table is set for seven people not six. Thinking surely she wouldn't make a mistake like that, she checks with her husband; he hasn't been in the dining room, he assures her. At a loss, Sally removes the seventh place setting.

Later, Sally returns again to the table with candles and there are seven place settings. She knows for sure this time that she only laid six. She checks again with her husband. He hasn't been in the room. Feeling uneasy,

Sally removes the cutlery and mat from the seventh setting and puts it away.

As diner, that night, is coming to an end, Sally relays the story of Mrs Wilson and the flowers. She points to the flowers on an oak cabinet in the corner of the room. She tells them about the extra place setting and everyone begins asking questions.

Eventually her friend Vicky says, "Perhaps it's the ghost. Have you thought about that?"
Sally had but didn't want to admit it, "That's madness. Why would a ghost be here?"
"For his flowers," replies Kate dramatically.
Sally blanches, "You don't think?"
"Could be, I suppose," William leans back in his chair, "How else could it have happened? We were the only two here, and I didn't do it."
Sally looks at the flowers long and hard. "You're right. There was no one else here."

Everyone around table is watching Sally intently and she feels her face flush. Kate sniggers first. Vicky kicks her under the table and they can no longer hold in their secret, they laugh out loud. Sally is confused when everyone joins in.

Vicky has the key to Sally and William's house. She never returned it from the summer, when they were on holiday and she used it to water the plants. William told Vicky about the flowers and she'd sneaked in while Sally was busy in the kitchen. "Thank God for that." Sally gives a heavy sigh and joins in the laughter.

A loud bang on the wall in the corner of the dining room stops the hilarity instantly. Everyone looks towards the sound, then back at each other; scanning faces to see if this is another joke.

A translucent, grey misty hand with twisted, arthritic fingers is grabbing at the air as it moves through the wall. Hearts pound and a chill spreads through the room. Sally feels a cold sweat, sticky on her back. Her stomach lurches catching her breath. The three men in the company jump up, scraping their chairs behind them, and run for the front door - with shouts to the girls to stay where they are.

As William pulls the front door open and runs out of the house he is closely followed by Sid and Jake.

The three girls don't look at each other. They are too afraid to take their eyes off the disembodied hand. Fear floods their muscles as their jaws hang loose.

A picture, hanging on the wall, behind them jolts and rattles against the exposed brick. They all swing round to look at the picture just in time to see it fly, unaided, off the wall. It flings itself across the room, hurtling over the dining table and crashes hard against the cabinet with flowers, in the corner. Glass shatters into pieces and scatters across the floor.

The men return, out of puff and sweating, fighting to get their breath back. William doubles over resting his hands on his knees and begins to announce that there is no one outside but stops mid-sentence; they all stare at the broken picture and glass shards, splintered and piercing the wooden floor.

Shaken, William cleans up the broken glass, as Sally pours stiff drinks to calm everyone. They all return to the table and discuss animatedly what has just happened and possible causes; talking erratically over each other.

In the middle of the jittering conflab, an orchid lands on the table in front of Sally. She gasps and her heart threatens to sprint from her chest. Silence falls as everyone gawps wide-eyed at the single white flower. They look at Sally and at the flowers in the corner. One by one, orchids rise up from the wreath and sore across the room. A single white flower lands on the table at each of the occupied place settings. Terror spreads like a disease and the evening comes to an abrupt end, at that very precise moment.

The next time Sally sees Mrs Wilson, she is cagy at first as he tries to tell her what happened. Then the whole story spills out in a flurry. Mrs Wilson laughs; "Oh no, Mr Wilson really was a strange man. He hated being left out of things but his biggest bug bare is he hated people borrowing things and not returning them. He couldn't stand it; it used to drive him to distraction. I blame his mother. He couldn't share either; that's why we had to bury him in the back garden."

Sally's face is waxy as she shivers and perspiration soaks in to her tunic. She is washed out and eager to finish up. As she continues with Mrs Wilson's hair, she mentally vows never to accept any gifts from a customer again.

Mrs Wilson happily checks her hair in her mirror when Sally is finished. They chat, relaxed about incidentals and possible upcoming holidays. Sally picks up a hair brush and twiddles with it as she is listening to Mrs Wilson talk about her planned trip to Italy on a luxury train. She always thought she would have to wait until Mr Wilson was dead, as he would never go with her.

Sally packs away her things, giggling. As she does, she puts the hair brush she's holding into a box in the trolley. A hair brush which Mrs Wilson always uses. The hair brush Mr Wilson no longer has a use for.

Butterflies with Batwings

It has been an hour so far but it seems longer. I feel I'm on the end of a losing battle with the wind, which is abrasive for this time of year. My fingers are red and painfully stiff from the cold. I have no pockets, no shelter for them, so I just clench my fists and stride on.

The rucksack on my back was manageable at first but with each stride up the hill, I feel it pressing harder and harder into my shoulder blades. I removed it a few times to adjust the contents, in the hope it would offer me some relief. All my efforts were in vain and I know I will just have to put up with it.

I put my head down to protect my burning cheeks from the singing force, which makes my eyes sting and leak. My tears feel warm on my chilled face. My hair keeps blowing into my mouth and over my eyes and I have nothing to tie it back with. I had carefully styled it this morning. Even though he won't appreciate it, I still want to look my best. But I know my eye make-up will be streaking its way towards the top of my cheek bones. I'm going to be a soggy mess by time I get there.

I look up occasionally to gauge the distance to go. Blank ink has been thrown over the sky and is beginning to permeate its way through any blue that was present earlier. I hate storms, although I know the rain will make the ground softer.

The trees are my marker, as they are the gateway to the ruin where Si would be waiting for me. They stand about half a mile away now. When I had set off on this expedition, they had looked like two magnificent pieces of broccoli sprouting out the ground. They were a perfect shade of fresh, vegetable, green with a purple blue hue, which seeped into the, then, clear blue sky above them. Now they are animated, soft, leafy creatures, dancing rhythmically in time with the steady gusts of wind that are getting stronger.

The landscape is rugged and the rough un-manicured grass is kept at bay by a few ragged sheep I can now see clearly, in small groups. Any other day this place would have struck me as beautiful. The vastness of it is breath-taking. No human interference, save the grey stones protruding from the ground, like broken bones emerging through torn flesh; bones which once sheltered the heart of a home. Perhaps it was a small holding, with children laughing and playing while a mother and father worked long days tending the land. It was now just a ruin, reminiscent of a time long ago and of yesterday's *unforeseen* events.

My need for shelter is now pressing; I can hear the faint drumming of thunder in the distance. It is getting closer and I know soon I'll be standing under a whole orchestra. The rain begins. My feet are becoming heavy to lift, sodden with wet mud. Pins and needles shoot into my face, my long hair now pasted to my cheeks. I have no choice but to carry on.

The ruin is almost upon me. I will actually reach my destination in good time, despite the weather's attempts to delay me. The reality of my predicament makes my stomach lurch a few times and I try to dismiss negative thoughts and concentrate on what I have to do when I reach Si. I always get nervous when I meet up with him but this was something else. I have butterflies with bat wings. I stop for a moment. I look towards an opening in the ruin, which would have been a window or a doorway once upon a time. I sense movement.

I hear myself gasp. This is unexpected. Why is there movement, is it him? I hold my breath until I realise it's just a few sheep huddling together for shelter. I wait a few more seconds to be sure then, proceed. I think I'll have to shoo them away when I get there, as they will get in the way. I don't want any eyes on us, even if they are just animals.

Yesterday I couldn't wait for his warm, strong arms to wrap me up; for his breath on my face, and to feel his intense pleasure inside me. It all just went so wrong in a heartbeat.

The trees finish dancing and are now bowing over and over again … is it in honour of *their* dance performance, or from fear of my presence? I drop my heavy load and hold my head up to the full force of the rain, bracing myself. I pull open the loosely tied chord of my rucksack and holding firmly onto the wooden handle, I drag the rest of the spade out into the wet.

As I enter the ruin I can see him sitting up against a large moss shrouded rock where I'd left him. I thought he would be bloated maybe, or show some signs of decay but he doesn't look a lot different, apart from his face. He is a mottled blue-grey colour, which makes him look like his skin has been wrapped in latex - translucent and silky from the rain. Because he is in the same sitting up position, I would have to see how malleable he is. Chances are, rigor mortis would have set in and I will have to dig deeper, rather than long, to fully conceal his 6ft 2 bulk.

I had thrown his jacket over his lap before I ran down to the village last night to conceal his … situation. I remove it now, to reveal his *still* erect penis! How could he still have a hard-on? I immediately question his *deadness* and take a step back to assess him.

Of course he is dead. I stabbed him in the ear with a cork screw and strangled him with my scarf. The cork screw is still sticking out! Most of the blood has washed away with the rain but thicker clots still cling to his neck like leaches. The front of his shirt, where his gushing blood had congealed overnight is fluid again, pouring down into his exposed lap.

A sudden surge of panic thrusts me back to the memory of yesterday's romantic picnic. Butterflies are hurling themselves around my gut. I was sure he was going to propose. We had some wine and we were having sex against the rock. Just as he was about to … he called me Angela … well … who the fuck is Angela?

I have to decide where to dig, then what to do with the spade, my bag, my clothes and shoes. The killer always gets found out on the telly and I need to cover my tracks very carefully.

My shoe prints … not sure what to do about those. I might have to keep coming up here and run about in loads of different pairs of shoes in various sizes. Fucking ridiculous! Why had I not thought about my footprints!

I start to dig. God I'm knackered after just a few minutes and the ground has just turned into brown slush and keeps sliding back into the hole. I move spots twice, as Si has shit himself and the sweet sickly smell is making me feel ill. It isn't his fault but it's very frustrating.

Five hours on and I think I'm done. I've drunk a litre of water and I'm now bursting for a wee, so I go to the corner of the ruin to relieve myself. When I stand up I see watery movement coming up the hill towards us. I can make out four, maybe five figures, getting closer and smaller blobs which are moving faster. Much faster … Shit! They're dogs! I pull my trousers up with shaking hands. The adrenalin makes me forget how cold and numb they are.

If I run, they'll see me. I quickly try and drag the mannequin of Si, into the grave, which has now pooled into a mud bath from the relentless storm.

I can't bloody shift him. I can hear the dogs barking. They are really close. I slump down next to Si even though he stinks and looks more grotesque with each passing minute. I could say I found him like this but how do I explain this hole, or his penis? And, the cork screw will have my fingerprints all over it!

If only you had called out *my* name, we would have been married by July!

Phantom

You check the clock on the wall. It has been just over an hour since you left the hospital. You sit in your bath, in too much pain to lie back and let the warm water sooth you. You check the clock again. It's nearly 3pm. If you leave it any longer you could be in trouble. No point in ringing for an ambulance yourself, or going to the GP again; that had always proved to be a waste of time, just like it had again today.

Why had she called in the practice nurse and asked you to sit in the waiting room, while they discussed your *situation*? What were they saying that you were not allowed to hear? Why were the receptionists speaking in hushed voices and looking over at you mockingly? They reluctantly called an ambulance when you started crying and vomiting with the pain; they had said as much. *Just to be sure* the GP had told the ambulance crew but they all seemed to be sure it was nothing physical. Again.

The paramedics were offhand. You knew they wanted to call you a time waster; tell you others needed their help more. They offered you paracetamol but nothing stronger. They said they needed you 'lucid' for an appropriate assessment?

Why did the hospital not call someone down from maternity, or gynae, to check you over? Why did they assume it was the same as before? Why would no one take you seriously? The doctor said he remembered you from the last time. You didn't tell him you had been in two more times since then. You noticed his surgical blues were creased. His young face was tired and his hair had not been combed. He took your blood, and told you he knew it would show nothing untoward, as he knew your *situation*. He was too young for such cynicism and you told him so. What did he know about life; about *your* life!

His tired eyes became more wearisome, as you pleaded to be listened to, as you pleaded for your sanity. Nurses came in to offer support but it was him they were supporting. When you became hysterical, they left you alone. They made calls. You knew they were seeking wisdom from medics, who would not be armed with the help you actually needed. You knew you would end up strapped to a bed again, until you told them what they wanted to hear; until you denied the truth of *the situation.* So you ran. You ran home.

At three months, you were told your home test had given a false positive. All 14 of them? Your husband believed you at first, like he always had. But he couldn't see what you saw. No-one could. Even when you pointed out the head and the fingers; they saw nothing but an empty void on the scan. You saw everything especially their pity and frustration.

You craved olives and ice cream, as you had the time before; and you couldn't stomach fish, like the time before that. Your belly grew this time, u*nlike* all the times before. And, you felt it move. Like nothing you had *ever* felt before.

He left you. He said he was lost without you … because *you* had lost your mind. For months you tried to prove them all wrong. Online searches, chat lines and forums offered some hope; and a friendship group in the US, for women like yourself, who were also, wrongly, told they were 'moms' to *never* be.

Pointless and humiliating visits to casualty, at different times of the day and night, were journeyed. You needed to find one paramedic, one nurse, or one doctor who would believe you. You only needed one.

Thinking you were in labour you got into your bath. What else could it be? You had read many times that water is a natural anaesthetic and you needed some reprieve, as there was no other relief on its way. No midwife would come knocking. You cried out. Low moans at first but then screams. Drunk with exhaustion and the excruciating waves of the unrelenting contractions, you noticed the bath water change colour. Blood. You felt faint but managed another scream; for help. You felt pressure between your legs and an overwhelming urge to bear down. You were breathing fast and your heart was pounding.

You heard the drumming in your ears. As another wave ripped through your abdomen you were aware you were losing control as the pain took over. You pulled out the plug and watched, as the darkened water began to swirl away. You gathered your strength and attempted to stand. You were pushing down again. Screaming.

You felt a burning, tearing sensation, as you stepped out of the bath. You strained, as you squatted down with urgency. Still shouting for someone to hear, to come, to help, you pushed again; the pressure was unbearable. Something warm slipped between your thighs and fell out, away from you, onto the bathmat below. Just as everything turned black you were aware that someone else, maybe more than one person, had entered the room. And you heard a baby cry.

Loud clattering jolts you awake, something moving along? You think it's a trolley, as the sound becomes more definite. You are aware that you are lying down. You remember you had been in your bathroom. The pain in your pelvis has gone. What had that been? Are you still on your bathroom floor? No, too soft. A bed. The trolley sound stops, nearby. You can hear someone talking, it is quiet but it's the deep tone of a man. A woman talks next. What are they saying; are they talking about you? The voices are too muffled, you can't make out the words; it's as if they are on the other side of a wall.

You try and open your eyes but they are too heavy. You drift in and out of consciousness. You dream you are in pain. You dream you are giving birth alone. You remember. You remember the baby crying! Adrenalin jump starts your heart and your eyelids spring open. You want to sit up but you can't lift your arms, something has clasped them down by your sides! You look around, frantic, breathless … helpless. Your wrists and ankles are tied down with straps, on a bed, in a room you recognise but it's not a room in your house.

"No! No! No! Not again … please, no!" You can't believe this is happening and you cry for your baby, your new born baby.

The voices rush to you. They are in tunics. Medical people! For a split second you believe they will help you but the man holds you still. You are begging again, pleading to be heard. To be believed. Someone has stolen your baby. You know it now. You remember it all with clarity. Your cries fall as you are given an injection of something that makes your arm cold. You can't fight anymore.

The nurse is trying to sooth you. She strokes your hair. She tells you it will be ok … *it always is*. The man asks why you are so distressed. *You* want to tell him.

You want *him* to believe you. You want him to know you were pregnant. You want him to listen and to be horrified to hear that you have just delivered a baby, alone, unassisted and it was taken from you. Taken by strangers in your house!

You open your mouth but the sedation has rendered you speechless. Tears fill your eyes and spill over onto your pale cheeks. The woman tells him you have been in hospital for 28 years, following a series of traumatic miscarriages and phantom pregnancies. You hear her. You take in your surroundings. You know this place. You understand.

But the baby. Where is your baby?

Filthy, Dirty Pig

The sudden pain was excruciating as teeth clamped around his leg. He kicked out, nothing could make the pig loosen his grip. Sharp yellow teeth tore into his calf. Blood seeped through his jeans like ink on cartridge paper. He kicked out again. The pig was frenzied, rabid. He felt the rise of acid and bile in his throat.

Luke slumped to the ground and rolled on to his front. He could taste the shit and swill in the pen as his breathing deepened. Warm puke forced from his stomach splashed down in front of him. The smell hit his nostrils and another surge of vomit was ejected from his gut. The pig's grip was relentless and tightened as Luke wriggled and thrashed in his bid to escape. He screamed as his shin bone snapped and searing pain shot though his leg.

The ringing in Luke's ears was deafening as he fought unconsciousness; he had to stay awake, he had to stay alive.

His own screams masked the sound of the pig grunting and snorting as it ravaged him. Luke watched in agonising horror as the pig sheered the muscled from his lower limb. Adrenalin pumped and provided renewed strength. He yanked his leg away from the raging creature, trying to release the animal's hold. His efforts were in vain. He gave way to hysteria as the pig ripped his foot from his leg.

The blood engorged porcine backed away, carrying his prize in his mouth. The dirty, filthy pig looked like a malevolent, mutant clown with its cheeks and snout smeared in blood. He retreated to the corner of the pen with Luke's dismembered foot.

Terror immobilised Luke as he haemorrhaged; blood spurted from the mutilated stump in rhythm with his racing heart. He strained, lifting his head to look;

barely able to keep his chin from dropping back down into the rancid dirt where he lay. The loss of blood, exhaustion and shock dragged him closer to death.

The other pigs looked on.

Luke shook and his vision blurred. Through a haze he saw the pig coming towards him again. It walked slowly, with its head raised, as if proud, powerful; like it had done, moments before it attacked him. He panicked and tried to prepare himself for a second thrashing but he was too weak to defend himself. As the animal drew close, Luke feared he was going to die.

Luke felt overwhelmingly cold as his blood drained from the open wound and he shivered uncontrollably, as he drifted in and out of consciousness. The pig appeared, altered. It was no longer a pig. Luke wasn't conscious enough to take this in. Was he hallucinating? The pig, what was the pig, walked on two feet; a man, but not human. His grey skin could be seen through the dark layer of blood. Luke's blood. The creature's mouth grimaced and held the same yellow, razor sharp teeth as the pig. Fresh chunks of tissue and deoxygenated blood dripped in front of him, as he swaggered over to Luke lying helplessly on the ground. Small tusks, protruded from either side of its nose. A lump of torn flesh, skewered on the end of one tusk, dislodged and splatted on the ground, as it continued to advance towards Luke. It didn't notice. Its eyes were fixed solely on Luke's mutilated body.

The other pigs were distressed, agitated; they began to shake and whimper as they stood together in a huddle. One look from the man, with a flick of his fiery, orange eyes, and they were silent. Luke began to crawl towards the pigs but he didn't believe anything would keep him safe.

The inhuman moved slowly, controlled. His sickly grin spread across his face and he cackled when Luke began to move. Luke tried to slither along the ground, squelching. The man opened his mouth.

"Here little piglet, come to Papa!"

Luke couldn't understand. It was his father's voice, but this didn't look like anything like his father.

He curled himself into a foetal position amidst the warm, sweaty stench of the pigs, with blotches of dried mud and vomit on their pink and black skin. They offered some camouflage, comfort even, but they were scared, he sensed it. He couldn't stifle his cries any longer;

"Please … please don't …"

The disgusting abomination laughed. The hideous, repugnant, non-human shrill, reverberated into the night and ripped into Luke's soul. He lost control of his bowels and felt bile rise in his throat again.

The pig-man squealed to the pigs. One by one they shuffled forward …

Authors' note: 'Filthy, Dirty Pigs' has two endings, both are published here Please choose which you prefer.

Ending one

The creature stopped in its tracks. It sensed company. In haste, the farmer leaped into the pen and flung open the gate to the other sty. He hadn't seen the horror that lurked in the shadows; he'd only heard the commotion and assumed it was the grey at the centre of it.

"Is it the grey one? We should have sold him way back … what did I say!" his wife chided, as she ran to help. "Not now! Christ, it isn't the time for 'I told you so'! Get that pig in isolation! I'm going to get my rifle. This ends now!"

She could just barely make out the creature, now poised in an indignant stand-off with her. Before she could rationalise what was happening, the bulk pushed into her. She screamed and lost her footing falling backwards into the filth.

As she tried to stand, the angry beast turned and charged at her again; piercing the air with its shrill squeals and rabid grunts. It knocked her back against the fence with its full force. The man-pig's yellow, blood ensanguined teeth were set to bite down. She could feel the animal's breath on her face; the fetid smell made the contents of her stomach curdle. She realised there was no escape and braced herself for the inevitable. She called for her husband but the pig's snarling teeth sawed down into her torso, tore and ripped at her guts, which poured out onto the ground in front of her. The pain lasted only a few seconds.

Luke was struggling to take in each breath. He'd heard the man-pig's sickening laughter from somewhere close by. He strained his neck to see into the other sty where the pig was ready to charge again. To charge at him.

Their eyes locked. A deafening 'crack' and then another, reverberated around the sty. The abomination fell to the floor like a giant slab of fatty, blood-saturated meat. It was over.

The farmer raised the rifle, so the butt was at his shoulder and his finger was light on the trigger. He took aim and Luke could see tears, which glinted on the farmer's cheeks in the moonlight, like streaks of glitter. Just as he went to squeeze the trigger, two pigs appeared, as if from nowhere and snuffled towards

Luke. Back to back they stood and intertwined their tails, sealing themselves into a protective wall. The farmer shouted at them to move as something large emerged in front of him, obscuring the view of his target. A sharp burning pain in his neck and shoulder rendered him almost unconscious. He saw the shape of his bloody, ragged arm drop to the ground and heard a 'snap!' as his body broke under the force of sharp teeth.

"And that's how we came to inherit the farmhouse."

"What happened to Luke?" the boy looked younger than his fourteen years.

"Oh, Luke was saved by the two pigs that shielded him. They protected him for a few years after that."

"And the man-pig thing? The creature?"

"No one knows. Drink your milk. You need fattening up."

The boy laughed nervously. "None of this is *true*. There's no such thing as a man-pig that eats humans …"

"And, pigs. Don't forget he loved to eat pigs, too."

The boy felt a bit unwell. The graphic tale had upset him but he didn't want to show his father just how much.

"Can I go over to the fire, dad, I feel cold?" The boy heaved himself up with his bony hands and reached for a wooden crutch leaning against the table. His one foot took the weight of his scrawny body as he levered his way over to the open fire.

He glanced back at his father who was watching him struggle. The flames of the candlelit room reflected an orange hue from his father's eyes; his bushy moustache protruded from his sallow skin like small pointed tusks. The boy's heart began to thump in his chest and he was sure his father could hear it.

"Where are the two pigs that protected Luke?" He felt nauseous, as fear gnawed at his stomach. He had felt like this before, a long time ago but couldn't remember why.
His father grinned, sickly yellow, at the boy.
"Dead, Luke. The pigs are both dead now …"

Ending two

One Hampshire pig was close; it snorted and snuffled into Luke's neck, nuzzling. It's rough, leathery skin provided a welcomed warmth like a horse hair blanket. It opened its mouth and he felt its stale breath warm on his cheek.

In one swift movement it clamped its teeth in to the base of Luke's skull. Pain wrecked through his body sending a shudder into the night. Luke, torn and battered, convulsed and his muscles drove ridged in spasm; his limbs tensed and stretched like meat hanging from the butchers hook. He shrieked as the pig snapped his spine. He was paralysed from the neck down, immediately, while his scream hung in the air.

The other pigs surrounded him and bit into his flesh. Ripping. Tearing. Pulling. Feeling nothing but numbness, Luke watched in horror. Blood spurted as the pigs feasted making light work of stripping his flesh.

The smallest of the sounder of swine, unable to join in the festivities, ventured near to Luke's head. It looked him in the eye with confusion, seconds before it severed his nose from his face. An explosion of blood filled Luke's throat and the pain crucified him. Luke was catapulted down a dark tunnel. The pig-man, reached in to his chest. The last thing Luke saw, before the darkness took him, was his father bite into his heart.

Morning broke and Luke woke aching and cold in the sty, covered in mud and excrement. His head pounded, he was confused, and his skin was clammy and grey.

He saw his Mother approach, banging a metal bucket with a stick to signal feeding time. She stopped, her mouth gaped open. She called out his name and he looked directly at her. His mother screamed and fell to her knees with tears running down her face. *"I warned you! Didn't I warn you? For God's sake! Over and over, I told you never turn your back on the grey one."* She wailed and it echoed around the farm.

"I told you! You don't want to go like your father did, he's a swine." His Mother bellowed.

Luke raised himself to all fours. He couldn't make the final leap to two feet; his cumbersome bulk prevented him.

Luke shook uncontrollably and his breathing became difficult and laboured, his heart pounded, thunder clapped in his temples. He panicked, scared. He didn't know what he'd done wrong and he backed away from his Mother. He sought solace with his Father. Close together, the two grey pigs squealed and shuffled backwards, their small black tails entwined; united and twisted.

Please let us know which ending you choose by leaving a review on Amazon.
We'd love to hear from you.

About the Authors

Jessica Fairfax has lived most of her life in the North East of England. She spent years working in the Public Sector within the Youth Justice System and as a Senior Manager writing and delivering courses for parents, carers and children. She has a Psychology Degree and was a Primary School Teacher.

Jessica writes under various pseudonyms and is a published poet. Her work appears in a number of anthologies including 'Traveller's Moon' and 'God Created Women' by Aural Images both available on Amazon.

Jessica is interested in the human psyche and parapsychology. She enjoys reading horror, paranormal and crime fiction. Jessica's stories are cleverly constructed from a mixture of real life experiences and her vivid imagination. Her writing takes the reader on a journey to very dark places and makes the unimaginable believable.

As well as collaborating with Carol Walker on various projects, she also writes individually and is currently working on her first crime thriller with a paranormal sub plot.

Carol Walker was born and bred in Newcastle, where she went to college and trained as an Art Director. She worked creating campaign ideas and designs for clients nationally. She has had a varied back ground including Lecturing in Design, Internet Production and IT Management.

She has a long held interest in psychology and people; trying to understand what makes them tick. Her passion lies in psychological thrillers and crime fiction. This has heavily influenced her writing. Carol writes captivating and gripping stories and she has a flare for scaring reader in a very plausible and imaginative way.

As well as writing with Jessica Fairfax on various projects, including this anthology, she writes independently and is currently working on her first crime novel.

23442170R00112

Printed in Great Britain
by Amazon